WILD

Monkey Magic

LUCY COURTENAY

Hodder
Children's
Books

A division of Hachette Children's Books

More books by Lucy Courtenay

WILD
1. Tiger Trouble

Coming soon . . .
3. Bear Hug
4. Koala Crazy

More from Hodder Children's Books

THE PONY WHISPERER
The Word on the Yard
Team Challenge
Runaway Rescue
Prize Problems
Pony Rebellion
Stables SOS
Janet Rising

Saffy's Angel
Indigo's Star
Permanent Rose
Caddy Ever After
Forever Rose
Caddy's World
Hilary McKay

Foreword

by Chris Brown,
Director of Tooth 'n' Claw

*The UK's premier animal training facility
for Film, TV and advertising.*

Keeping wild creatures in your home, like Taya and
Tori, may seem to be entirely insane and for the most
part this is true. It is totally impractical to have them
roaming the house, destroying the furniture and
shredding your clothes. I too grew up in a home full of
wild animals. When our lions weren't chewing or
chasing the dog, the chimps would steal all the biscuits
and the bear would climb up the curtains. The python
would sleep through the chaos only emerging to eye
the cat hungrily – which was the cue to feed him
another frozen mouse. Luckily for us, we never had a
house fire to contend with as well!

The jammy dodger breath of a chimp waiting
patiently inches from my nose for me to wake up will
live with me for ever. It is a heck of an upbringing and
I would not have missed it for the world.

www.toothnclaw.com

A Catalogue record for this book is available from the British Library

ISBN-13: 978 1 444 90139 9

Typeset in AGaramond by Avon DataSet Ltd,
Bidford on Avon, Warwickshire

Printed and bound by CPI Group
(UK) Ltd, Croydon, CR0 4YY

The paper and board used in this paperback by Hodder Children's Books
are natural recyclable products made from wood grown in
sustainable forests. The manufacturing processes conform to the
environmental regulations of the country of origin.

Hodder Children's Books
a division of Hachette Children's Books
338 Euston Road, London NW1 3BH
An Hachette UK company
www.hachette.co.uk

For my goddaughter Olivia.

*With special thanks to Chris Brown of
Tooth 'n' Claw and John Pullen,
Curator of Mammals at Marwell Zoo.*

Prologue
Moments of Great Shock

'Did our house just blow up?'

I think it was me who asked the question. Although maybe it was my twin, Tori. At moments of great shock, it's sometimes hard to work out whether I'm remembering my own stuff or my sister's. I'm pretty sure my mouth moved. It may have just screamed. Or maybe it really did find words. Who knows?

Right now, the last thing I feel like doing is explaining how Tori, Mum, Joe Morton and I had come to be standing at our back gate with Rabbit, our ancient golden retriever, and two six-month-old Bengal tiger cubs on leads, watching our house burning down. So you'll forgive me if I don't give you too many details. Stick with me and it'll get clearer. Just then, nothing was very clear to me either.

Smoke was still rising; flames poked hot orange tongues at the sky. I kept staring at the place where I'd last seen our chimneys and our roof through the trees of Fernleigh Common. Perhaps if I moved sideways a bit more, I'd see the house. It couldn't have blown up. It was impossible.

The noise from the explosion had terrified the tiger cubs, Chips and Gravy. They were making the most awful growling noise, their round orange ears flattened to their heads and their lips curled back in the scariest expressions you ever saw. They were pacing in circles, crouched low to the ground, yowling softly and moving in this flowing way that made me think of oil glugging out of a bottle. Somehow, our friend Joe was still holding on to their leads.

'DID OUR HOUSE JUST BLOW UP?'

That was definitely me. The noise made my throat hurt.

Rabbit laid her heavy yellow head back on her shoulders and howled. Dwight Dingle and his gang, who'd been chasing us only moments before, had disappeared. Sirens wailed out on the main road. People started to appear from everywhere, hurrying across the common, rushing out of their gates, joining us where we stood gazing at the place where our house had been standing right up until approximately a minute ago. Hardly anyone glanced at the cubs. You'd think a pair of six-month-old tigers on leads would make people stare. But apparently exploding houses were more interesting.

'Mum,' Tori whispered, 'is Dad still in there?'

That was the bit when Mum started screaming.

1

Completely Freaky

Mum raced towards our back gate. 'ANDY!' she screamed. 'ANDY!'

My feet were glued to the ground. I couldn't have moved if I wanted to. *My dad was in the house.* Except there *was* no house. So— My brain stopped working right there.

'ANDY! ANDY!'

Grown-ups on phones stood all around, talking urgently. Tori made a dash after Mum. Someone grabbed her and tugged her back.

'Don't go down there, love—'

'Let me go!' Tori screamed, struggling. 'My mum! My dad!'

Bubbles of snot were pouring from my twin's nostrils

as she wept and yelled. Somewhere in my frozen brain, I could see that this was all wrong. *I* was the flaky idiot in the Wild family. Going mad and screaming and shouting was *my* job. But I wasn't doing it, and Tori was. Since my throat-burning yell, I'd turned into a piece of stone.

My twin sister and I might look the same with our long brown hair, brown eyes and pale English skin, but we aren't. Tori never cries. Tori always keeps her head in a crisis. She's way cleverer than me, all top marks in class while I plait my hair and wait to be told the answers. She knows more about *Doctor Who* than the average eleven-year-old girl. She is also the most sarcastic person I know, and sharpens herself on me when I lose the plot, which I often do. Watching Tori blubbing was completely freaky. But then so was watching my house explode.

Everything was different.

'Taya! Taya?' Tori fell into me, desperate for me to tell her it was fine and our house hadn't just blown up and Dad was in CostQuik down the road and not blown up as well. 'Dad's not dead!' she yelled. 'He can't be dead!' Then, in a move worthy of me on a really indecisive day: 'What if he's dead? Taya, what if they both die?' And then, probably due to the shock: 'My *Doctor Who* collectibles!'

I patted her numbly and tried not to picture Mum and Dad in flames. I couldn't think past that. Why wasn't I crying?

People had finally noticed the tigers. There was a ripple of nervous muttering as the cubs continued their soft, frightened growling. Still hanging on grimly to their leads, Joe threw a desperate look at me, trying to communicate sympathy and horror and what-should-I-do-with-the-tigers? all in the same look. He's the sort of boy who looks confused a lot of the time, with his big ears and his trousers that are a bit too short around his ankles. The confidence he'd shown as he faced Dwight Dingle and the bullies had gone. It belonged in a world where our house wasn't banging like a massive firework and my parents weren't in mortal danger.

Looking at my sobbing sister and Joe's helpless face, I realized that I, Taya Wild, the Queen of Shallow Things, was the only one close to holding it together right now.

I pushed my sister away, gently but firmly. *Don't think of Mum. Don't think of Dad.* 'Tori, cuddle the cubs. They're really scared.'

Tori dropped to the ground and pulled Chips and

Gravy in close, sobbing in a muffly way against their fur. The cubs' eyes were still wide and black and troubled, but they stopped their soft growling at her familiar smell. Rabbit started licking Gravy, comforting him in the only way a motherly old dog can. I turned my back on the flames as they shot up like rockets and mentally blocked my ears to the terrible roar.

'Joe, tie the cubs' leads to that tree.' *Don't think ...* 'We'll call Wild World. They're just across the common. They'll take the cubs in. We can borrow someone's phone – look up the number. We have to get them somewhere safe.'

'But what about your parents?' said Joe desperately.

I glanced back at the smoke and flames. Firefighters had arrived and jets of water were arcing into the middle of what was left of our house. A gust of wind swept the smoke into my eyes. I felt like something was burning me too. 'We can't help them just now,' I whispered. 'We can only help the cubs.'

The world tipped and wobbled. I shook my head, trying to clear it. But the world kept tipping. So I gave up and tipped too.

Days, hours, seconds later, I opened my eyes and

4

blinked at the strange ceiling over my head. It was speckled with little white lights.

Dad was sitting beside me. I was vaguely aware of the back of Tori scurrying out of the room as I took in more of my surroundings and realized I was in a hospital bed. I looked back at Dad. Everything rushed at me like a wall.

'Hello,' I said thickly. 'I thought you were dead.'

I sent a few messages down my arm, and my hand came up to prod gingerly at the bandage across the back of my head. 'Ow,' I said, surprised by how much it hurt. 'What did I do?'

'You fainted and knocked yourself out against a tree,' said Dad. He stroked my sweaty hair off my forehead.

'You didn't die,' I said, reaching out and gripping Dad's hand tightly in case this was all a dream and I was about to wake up.

'It takes more than an exploding house to get rid of me,' said Dad.

The careless way he spoke didn't match up with how he smelled of smoke and soot, nor the way his free hand was bandaged across his chest. His beard was a bit burned and his jumper was flecked with brown holes. I tried to remember whether the brown holes had been there before the fire or not, but gave up. Everything was still weird right now.

'What about Mum?' I sat up suddenly and winced. 'And the cubs?'

'Mum's fine and the cubs are safe at Wild World. Joe got someone to call just after you fainted, and they came within five minutes. How you thought of that . . .'

A proud look came in Dad's eyes. It made me feel warm and a bit embarrassed, but in a nice way.

Tori came back in with a clatter, towing Mum behind her. A doctor came too. I can't tell you how good it was to see Mum without flames shooting around her like I'd been imagining. She smelled of smoke too, and had a bruise on her dusty brown cheek and shiny tears in her big chocolate-drop eyes as she covered my face in kisses.

My sister shot me one of her unblinking gazes. Her hair, which had got a bit disordered when she was crying all over me, was pulled back into a fresh, neat ponytail. Her face, so totally exactly like mine, was calm. The wailing thing on Fernleigh Common had gone.

'You're not going to kiss me too, are you?' I checked cautiously. Kissing wasn't normally Tori's thing, but we weren't in the normal world any more.

'As if.' Her eyes dared me to remember her nutso performance on the common.

'How's your head?' asked the doctor, scribbling notes on a clipboard in her hand.

'Sore,' I said. 'But I'm OK.'

The doctor snapped the top back on to her pen. 'Any signs of dizziness or sickness, you should bring her back in straightaway,' she informed my parents. 'But you can take her home now.'

That was good, I thought in relief. I wanted to go home.

Then I remembered.

I looked at Mum and Dad. 'The house – is it . . . ?'

Dad took my hand. 'You'll have to be brave, Taya.'

There's nothing like being told to be brave to make you feel the opposite. You'd think that discovering the parents you thought had been burned alive were in fact *alive* alive would mean you could face most other things, wouldn't you? But not in my case. I felt sick, and that was before Dad gave me the really bad news.

'They're sifting through the rubble now, but it's not hopeful. It looks like we've got the van and the clothes we're in, and that's it.'

I gulped, trembling with the shock of hearing that I

had nothing to my name except a hideous school uniform, a bus pass and a bunch of biros in a dodgy school backpack. Then I turned to Mum. 'What about the snakes? Fernando and Sufi?'

Mum shook her head tearfully. She'd rescued Fernando and Sufi from a puffed-up twit who'd called himself a reptile-lover, but had somehow forgotten that snakes are cold-blooded creatures that need constant warmth. Their cages had been small and so cold that they had almost died of hypothermia until Mum brought them home to us. And now they were dead.

Mum loved animals. Furry, scaly, poisonous or cuddly – Mum understood and loved them all. She'd been fostering animal orphans for zoos and safari parks since before we were born, and Tori and I had spent our whole lives living with an assortment of creatures in need of Mum's special brand of TLC. Wallabies, monkeys, anteaters, snakes – and, most recently, Chips and Gravy the tiger cubs. Not your average pet assortment, but we're not your average family.

'What *happened*?' I said. 'Does anyone know?'

'They think it was a fault in the boiler,' Dad said. 'We'd only had the annual check two months ago, but there you go. There was a build-up of gas and . . . *boom*.'

I remembered the eggy smell in our kitchen that

morning. I thought it was . . . Never mind what I thought it was; it had been real gas, proper dangerous gas. *Boom*. A loud four-letter word that summed up the end of everything we'd ever known. Photos, furniture, clothes, carpets, saucepans, *Doctor Who* collectibles, a roof and four walls – all gone.

'At least we're all still alive,' said Mum into the silence. 'That is the most important thing.'

I struggled upright, trying to ignore my throbbing head. 'Bring it on, world,' I said, concentrating on keeping my voice as strong as I could. 'It'll take more than an exploding house to knock the Wilds down.'

Well. You have to stay positive, don't you?

2

Was it Well Hot?

News of the fire spread fast round Fernleigh, and we had offers to stay in people's houses. When I'd been checked out of hospital, Tori and I went to stay for a few nights with Zoe McGuigan – an old mate from our primary school, Castle Hill – while Mum and Dad stayed with our now ex-neighbour, Rob.

Zoe, Tori and I had only been at our different secondary schools for a couple of months – us at Forrests on the far side of town, and Zoe at All Hallows, the school where everyone from Castle Hill except us and Joe Morton had ended up – but it already felt like years. Zoe was perfectly nice and everything, but she kept asking questions that we really didn't feel like answering.

'You actually saw your roof come off?' she asked during supper on the first night we stayed there. 'In front of your eyes?'

'Please can you pass the ketchup, Mrs McGuigan?' said Tori loudly.

'In front of you?' Zoe repeated. 'Unbelievable!' And then she sat back in her chair with a wondering look in her wide blue eyes, as if she quite fancied seeing her own house blast off like a rocket.

'How's your new school, girls?' said Mr McGuigan in a hearty voice.

I glanced at Tori, but she didn't look back. I was grateful for the change of subject, but it was hard to know where to start with Forrests. Grey? Loud? A riot waiting to happen around every corner? Terrifying toilets and bullies on the bus?

'It's OK,' I said eventually.

'Zoe's having a great time at All Hallows, aren't you Zo?' said Mr McGuigan. 'She's already on the tennis team. And there's a trip to the French Alps coming up.'

'Our teacher's actually *French*,' said Zoe. 'She speaks French and *everything*.'

'I hear French people can do that,' Tori muttered, in a voice just loud enough for me to hear.

Tori and I had Mr Jones, who spoke French with a

Welsh accent and threw at least three kids out of the classroom every lesson. And not many kids played tennis because half the school rackets were broken. I prodded my lasagne and wished my head didn't hurt when I chewed.

'Does your mum still look after baby animals?' Zoe asked. 'Did any of them die in the fire?'

'We saw that newspaper article about your parents' new animal film business,' said Mr McGuigan. 'Terrific stuff. Hope they can still do it, what with – everything.'

I lost what little appetite I had. *Did* Mum still foster animal orphans? *Did* we still have an animal film business? Wild About Animals had only done one job so far, filming the tiger cubs in London. Now we had no house for the cubs – or any other animals – to live in. We had no weaning bottles, cages, heat lamps. There were no vitamins left, nor powdered milk. No teats, no incubator. Nothing.

'May we be excused, Mrs McGuigan?' I said, pushing back my chair.

'Of course . . . of course . . .' Zoe's mum rushed to help me and Tori out of our seats like we were a couple of old ladies. 'You must be tired. I've put a double mattress on the floor in Zoe's room. I hope that's OK?'

'You can tell me more about the fire tonight,' Zoe called after us brightly as Tor and I headed for the stairs. 'It must have been well hot to destroy totally everything you ever owned! Was it? Was it well hot?'

We didn't have to go to school the next day, which was a relief. The thought of all the questions from our classmates, like Zoe's only times thirty, was enough to send anyone screaming for a nice dark broom cupboard.

'But you have to go tomorrow,' said Dad as Mum drove us all to Wild World to check on the cubs. 'You've already had several days off school this term and you can't keep missing lessons.'

'But our house just exploded!' I said. 'They won't expect us back for *ages*. I mean, haven't we got more important things to think about than school? Like . . . beds and a roof and stuff? *And* everyone will be staring at us and feeling sorry for us and it will be completely impossible to concentrate on anything!'

'You'll have to find a way,' Dad said.

It wasn't fair. We'd already had more than our share of bad luck since school started. Dad had been really ill before half-term, on a photography job in the Colombian jungle. He'd been flown home in a coma thanks to undiagnosed diabetes. His illness had changed our lives already: he couldn't fly around the world taking pictures of animals for a while because it was too hard for him to manage his medication while he was still learning to hold his insulin pen the right way up, so instead he'd started Wild About Animals. It had all been going so well, and we'd all just done a brilliant shampoo advert starring Chips and Gravy and Mum, but now . . .

'Can we still do Wild About Animals, Dad?'

Tori often asks the exact questions I'm thinking. But Dad didn't answer her because Mum had just turned into our road.

'Why are we going this way?' Tori said after a shocked second of silence.

'It's the quickest route,' said Mum in a funny voice.

It was over in a second as the van flashed past our gate. Although Tori had turned her head and was staring hard out of the opposite window, I had to look. I saw the remains of four walls behind lots of official 'do not enter' tape, piles of rubble and unidentifiable burned objects lying around. What was left of the apple trees in the front garden were burned and black like something out of a horror movie. Fire officers were still moving around the site, checking things.

And then we were past, and the left turn for Wild World was ahead of us. Mum was crying silently, both hands gripping the steering wheel. Dad reached across and put the indicator on for her.

Think about the cubs, I told myself as tears flooded down my cheeks. *Think about Chips's wise eyes and Gravy's big feet. Think of the way they smell and how they talk to us with their special vuvuving noise. Most of all think how, unlike poor Fernando and Sufi, they* didn't *die. And nor did we.*

3

Banana Smoothies

Wild World backs on to the other side of Fernleigh Common from our house, so in theory we could have walked the cubs straight up there ourselves in twenty minutes flat on the day of the fire. But Mum's spent years drumming it into us that the scrubbier parts of the common near Wild World can be dangerous if you're without a grown-up – there's an old quarry pit with steep sides and some funny boggy bits that can wreck your shoes and twist your ankles off. So I never thought of it.

Tori and I have been to Wild World about a million times because of Mum's fostering work. The animals have big enclosures, with the less dangerous ones like zebras and emus put in nice open fields. There are lots of mature trees, plenty of wide grassy areas for picnics and two excellent adventure playgrounds. Three long, modern buildings with moss-covered roofs stand in a cluster by the petting farm – these hold all the tropical creatures that need more warmth than an average day in Surrey provides. There's a lake for the sealions, a glass-fronted pond for the penguins and a cheerful, zebra-striped building which holds the shop and the café. A pebbly yellow track winds around the whole place for the little zebra-striped road-train to take people around.

As soon as we parked, Matt, the manager, came hurrying out to see us. He was a big man with a fat tummy that strained at his black-and-white Wild World polo-shirt and a big smile that went practically the whole way around his round red face. I think if I worked with animals all day long, I'd probably smile like that too.

'Good to see you,' Matt said, shaking Dad's hand and giving Mum a hug. 'Chips and Gravy are grand – both had a good night. They miss you, though.' He turned to us, raising his grey eyebrows. 'Which of you two thought of calling us, then?'

'Taya did,' said Tori, looking at the ground.

My sister had been a bit funny with me since the

fire. Not nasty, just quieter than normal. I looked sideways at her, trying to get her to look up and grin at me. But she kept staring at her feet.

'Smart thinking, Taya,' said Matt, patting me on the shoulder with a big red hand. 'How are you feeling? I hear the back of your head met a tree?'

I nodded, then wished I hadn't. My head still throbbed.

'Nasty,' Matt said sympathetically. 'Come along – the cubs will be pleased to see you! I'll take you up to the enclosure.'

'We'll walk,' said Mum, motioning at Rabbit panting beside her. 'Rabbit needs some exercise. You go with Dad and Matt, girls. You always enjoy the buggy.'

It was true. Matt's black-and-white electric buggy was fun. I felt more cheerful as I hopped in the back. Dad went in the front with Matt and Tori climbed silently in beside me.

The buggy moves dead slowly. It's nearly quicker to walk. But that's not the point. Matt drove us up the hill past a new wooden building I'd never seen before and then turned off through some trees towards the tiger enclosure. I glanced up at the trees – and then glanced again. They were enclosed by a high wire fence.

'There's never been a fence around those trees before,' I said, craning my neck to look upwards as we trundled along. I could see ropes slung among the branches now and some kind of wooden platform in a central clearing. 'Are you getting some new animals?'

'Chimpanzees,' said Matt.

I'm ashamed to say that all thoughts of my burned-down house and dead snakes and lost possessions flew out of my head. Chimpanzees! Actual chimpanzees!

'Chimps?' I squeaked. 'Seriously?'

'Absolutely.'

Even Tori was roused out of her funny brooding mood and started peering among the tree trunks. Wild World had never had chimps before. Mum had fostered a young chimp called Chestnut for a different zoo once, when Tori and I were about five. I could remember walking along the common with Mum with the little chimp on a lead, and how it had spooked a dachshund so badly that the poor dog had run up a tree in terror and got stuck.

'They were rescued from a laboratory in Asia and have been in quarantine in London for six months, waiting for their transfer here to Wild World,' Matt went on. 'Three males, two females. One of the females is expecting.'

Sometimes, I thought, I'd never understand the human race. I didn't want to think about what those people in Asia had been doing with five chimps in a laboratory, so instead I closed my eyes and thought about the bliss of a baby chimpanzee. Then I opened them again and eagerly scanned the trees for a glimpse.

'No good looking for them yet.' Matt grinned. 'One male and female arrived yesterday, but they're still inside getting used to their new ape-house. It's a learning curve for all of us, to be honest. We're waiting for the two other males and the pregnant female. Their flight was delayed into the country, so they've got a few more days of quarantine left before they can be moved. Shouldn't be long though.'

I pictured three chimpanzees sitting in a plane with seatbelts on, being offered banana smoothies by the stewardess. Then I giggled. It was really nice to laugh.

We were through the trees now and rolling past a little grassy turning on the left marked Greenings, which led to a house with two tall chimneys peeping over a big laurel hedge. The tiger enclosure loomed ahead of us. It was bright and open, with piles of rocks scattered about and a deep pond in the middle. Wild World's massive male, Sinbad, sat like a king on a rock by the wire fencing. It wasn't a thousand square miles of Bengali jungle, but Sinbad had been born and bred at Wild World, so he didn't know what he was missing. Two of his wives were prowling around the pond.

We waited about five minutes for Mum and Rabbit to come ambling through the trees, watching Sinbad as he flicked his tail majestically back and forth. Then we went to see the cubs.

Chips and Gravy were in a pen adjoining the main enclosure, so they could see Sinbad and his wives but not get into any fights. They were overjoyed to see us. Vuvuving frantically, they barged at Mum like two overgrown pussycats. Rabbit couldn't lick them fast enough.

'They're sending people from Sandown Safari and Yellowberry Park next week, to take them to their new homes,' Matt said as we fussed over them and tickled them in the spot behind their ears that they loved. 'They weren't expecting to take them for a couple more weeks, but given the circumstances . . .'

Thoughts of our ruined house loomed over us all again like a sad, smoky spirit. Matt cleared his throat and looked upset that he'd brought the subject up.

'Well,' he said a bit helplessly. 'Let's go and have a cup of tea, shall we?'

4

Well Hard with Capital Letters

'Why are you being so weird with me?' I demanded as Tori and I walked from Zoe's house to the bus stop the next morning. We'd endured another night of Zoe's questions – 'Are you like, really sad you lost everything?' – and I really hoped we wouldn't be staying there much longer.

'I'm not being weird,' Tori muttered.

'You are,' I said. 'You're all quiet. I need distracting.'

Tori made her special snorting noise. 'I'm sorry I haven't got anything to say, Taya, but our house just burned down so conversation isn't a big thing with me right now.'

'Don't you think I know that?' I fired back. 'I'm really sorry about your collectibles and everything,

Tor, but you're not the only one who's been affected, you know?'

'You think I'm worried about my *collection*?' Tori said.

'Well, you were wailing loudly enough about it on Monday,' I snapped.

Tori stopped dead. I actually felt quite scared by the look on her face.

'Forget I said that,' I said quickly.

The bus rolled up, thank wombats. My sister's prickly at the best of times, but at the moment she was like a ticking bomb.

It was a different stop from normal and the bus was fuller. Tori stormed on first. I waved my pass at the driver and scurried after her. Whispers and gasps followed us down the aisle.

Joe was sitting alone in his usual seat, his arms crossed firmly over his book bag. He jumped up when he saw us and looked so totally thrilled that his big ears blazed like bright-red beacons. Forrests had terrified Joe since the first day of term and he hated it when we weren't there. I think Tori and I were the only people who ever spoke to him. I had a feeling that his yesterday had been almost as difficult as ours.

'Oh my gosh, you're here!' He was practically

bouncing with excitement. 'I'm so glad to see you! I didn't think . . . I couldn't call you! And I didn't know where you were staying so I couldn't come round after school or anything! And now you're back! I'm so pleased you're here!' he repeated, as if not saying it several times would make me and Tor disappear in a puff of bus exhaust.

'Cheers,' I said glumly, squeezing past him and fishing a book out of my bag to hide behind. Tori sat silently on the other side of the aisle and stared straight ahead, ignoring all the pointing that was going on around us.

The bus swished back into the traffic.

'So, how are you?' said Joe.

'How was school yesterday?' I asked, sidestepping the question.

'Pretty bad,' said Joe honestly. He nodded at Tori, who was still gazing straight ahead with a face like a slab of granite. 'What's up with Tori?'

'She's well touchy at the moment,' I said. 'I think it's because she lost all her stuff in the fire.'

'You don't know anything.'

Tori was still staring straight ahead, but her words had been directed at me.

'Maybe that's because you've hardly said a word to

me since Monday!' I said, bristling. 'I'm not a mind-reader, Tori. I haven't got much to go on, you know?'

'Drop it, will you?' Tori snarled.

'Drop it?' I shouted. 'I didn't even start it! You should be grateful you're an only child, Joe,' I added furiously, swinging round to Joe so fast that he flinched. 'Sisters can be right cows.'

When we got to school, Tori didn't wait for me. She just bashed through the other kids and straight in the school gates like a long-haired geeky bulldozer.

'Talk to me while we're walking, yeah?' I said to Joe in a low voice. 'That way I can pretend everyone's not staring at me.'

Joe happily talked all the way from the bus to the classroom. It reminded me of when we first really met him, when he talked the back legs off a centipede – and the front ones too, come to think of it. I didn't take in half of what he was saying, but that didn't matter. At least I wasn't on my own. My thoughts raced to Tori. What was the *matter* with her?

In the classroom, my sister was already sitting down. I noticed that she'd taken a seat in a different part of the room so I couldn't sit next to her. Then I did a double take. She'd sat next to Cazza Turnbull.

Cazza was Well Hard with capital letters. She got in trouble most days, dyed her hair different colours and got a kick out of being horrible to everyone. The teachers hated her, but I thought she was the most interesting person in our year. She'd bullied us for a bit, but Tori had stood up to her on the bus one day and she'd been better since then. We still weren't best mates or anything, but she nodded wordlessly at me most mornings and no longer looked like she was going to kill me next time we were alone in the toilets. I still harboured hopes of being proper friends with her one day.

Seeing Tori next to the coolest girl in Year Seven knocked our argument out of my head for a minute. But as I tried to catch Tori's eye and waggle my eyebrows at her – meaning 'What are you doing next to Cazza?' – Ms Hutson, our class teacher, took me aside.

'We're all so sorry about the fire, Taya,' she said.

I mumbled something along the lines of 'Thanks, Miss,' and gazed down at the frayed bits of carpet on the floor.

'I gather no one was hurt?' she went on. 'That's good.'

Thoughts of Fernando and Sufi swam into my head.

'It's hard, I know, but things will get easier,' Ms Hutson went on. 'If you need extra time for your homework, or if you just feel you want to talk to someone, then let me know.'

'Really?' I said, looking up in surprise. Extra time for homework?

For a minute Ms Hutson looked human, not half android like we all suspected she really was. 'I've told your sister the same.' She looked over at where Tori was staring so hard at her new bit of table-top that I wondered for a minute if the whole table wasn't about to burst into flames. 'Tori's sitting somewhere different, I see?'

'I don't care where she sits,' I said loudly, so Tori would hear me.

'Interesting combination,' Ms Hutson said, almost to herself, as she gazed at Tori and Cazza. 'Well, sit down, Taya.'

There were two places left in the classroom: one next to Joe and one next to a boy called Biro. I'd never heard Biro speak. Sometimes I wondered if he had a tongue.

I sat next to Joe. Joe'd never had anyone sitting next to him in our form room before. When I put my bag down beside him, you could have plugged his smile into the wall socket and run Ms Hutson's whiteboard off it.

5

Sad, Sad Person

Ms Hutson slammed the register shut. 'Time to talk about the Christmas concert,' she said.

Everyone started groaning and putting their heads on their desks.

'Oh, Miss!'

'Do we have to, like, *sing*?'

When you're in Year Seven, groaning about a Christmas concert is the thing to do. Maybe everyone in the class was secretly going 'YIPPEE! We get to sing "Little Donkey"!' in their heads, but out loud they were groaning because they didn't want anyone to know they were secretly thinking this.

I looked around hopefully. If my so-called classmates were secretly excited, they were doing a good job of pretending a Christmas concert was the worst idea they'd ever heard.

'I like Christmas concerts,' I said defiantly to Joe, though I said it in a low voice.

'Me too,' said Joe. 'I used to sing in the church choir before Mum went. We sang all these carols . . .'

I felt bad for him as he stopped speaking and stared at the desk. It must be tough, having your mum walk out on you.

'Year Seven start the concert,' said Ms Hutson. 'All the classes together. Aren't we lucky?'

Everyone groaned even more loudly.

'And we're doing this,' Ms Hutson said. She reached round and pressed a button on the CD player behind her desk. The sound of a steel band burst out of the speakers, all funky and swaying. Everyone sat up, stunned.

'This isn't Christmas stuff, miss!'

'Keep listening,' said Ms Hutson.

A choir now started singing. I recognized the tune after about two seconds. It was that cheesy one, 'O Christmas Tree'. But I'd never heard it played like this before.

Half the class were now laughing.

'You have to be kidding, Miss.'

'No way are we singing that!'

I saw Tori lean over and whisper something at Cazza. Cazza looked thoughtful. Then she kicked back her chair, loud enough to get the class's attention.

'All *right*!' she said loudly.

It was like Cazza had just given everyone permission to be cool with this because almost at once, the whole of 7H started looking excited. *What a bunch of sheep!* I thought, relieved that it was now OK to grin enthusiastically. I caught Tori's eye, forgetting that I was mad with her. *What did you just say to make Cazza do that?* I tried to say in thought-waves. *Some kind of hypnotic mantra?* But Tori looked away.

'Wicked, Miss,' said one of the boys at the back, Jonno Nkobe.

'Are we doing the steel drums too?' said Heather Cashman, twirling one of her black curls around her finger the way she does when she's trying not to look too interested.

'A local band is coming to do the honours,' said Ms Hutson. She pressed a button on her keyboard and some words popped up on the whiteboard. 'O Christmas Tree,' she sang. 'O Christmas Tree, how lovely are your branches. Come on, 7H. Pretend you're on *The X Factor*.'

Like a herd of snorting buffalo, the class started mumbling the words. With Ms Hutson's encouragement, we grew a bit louder, then louder still, until we had something that sounded not totally awful. By the time we reached verse three, I noticed that the only person not singing was Biro. He sat staring at the ceiling, his eyes half closed, resisting all of Ms Hutson's pointed 'Come on! Everyone means *everyone*!' kind of remarks.

I glanced at Joe, swaying beside me with his arms outstretched and his eyes closed.

'What are you *doing*?' I hissed, mortified.

'Being a Christmas tree,' he said without opening his eyes. 'See my lovely branches?' And he waggled his fingers at me.

I shook my head. 'You are a sad, sad person.'

'Not bad for a first attempt,' said Ms Hutson as the song came to an end. 'We'll practise every Wednesday morning.'

I noted that no one groaned this time. Risking a glance across the room at Tori, I saw that she and Cazza had their heads together and were talking intently about something. All the Christmas fun faded away. I let my hair fall around my face like curtains and stared down at my desk, trying not to worry about the disturbing fact that Tori and Cazza seemed to be getting on like best mates.

Because where exactly did that leave me?

'Tori's spent a lot of time with Cazza today, hasn't she?'

'Yup.'

Joe and I were walking out of school at the end of the day. I'd hardly seen my sister since form room. Worms of fear wriggled in my brain. Had she left me for ever? Were she and Cazza now best mates? I was still wondering what Tori had said to get Cazza to make 'O Christmas Tree' acceptable to 7H. I also wondered what sort of conversation they were having right now.

'It must be rough, having Taya as your sister.'

'Yeah. And even worse that she looks like me. I can't pretend we're not related.'

'Hey, come back to my cool house and we'll listen to my extremely cool music and you can forget all about Taya.'

'Sounds great . . .'

'Isn't that your dad?' said Joe, pulling me out of my black thoughts.

I stared at the bearded bloke waiting by the gates. He was sweeping his eyes across the sea of grey jumpers that were pouring out of school down to the road, trying to spot me and Tor. It was probably like trying to pick two penguins out of a whole penguin colony. I was cheered to see Dwight Dingle and his gang shuffling away from their usual little-kid-kicking spot by the gate and glancing uncertainly at Dad, sensing the parent vibe.

'Taya!' Dad waved at me and nodded at Joe. 'Where's Tori?'

'With her new best friend, I expect,' I said.

Dad frowned. 'She's not with you?'

'I know it's weird, Dad,' I said, feeling cross, 'but Tori is weird right now. She's been like a nightmare since the fire. And now she's got a new mate and I don't know where she is or anything.' This last bit came out all quavery and strange.

'Ah,' Dad said in relief as Tori and Cazza walked up to us.

'Hi, Dad,' said Tori, shifting her book bag to a more comfortable spot on her shoulder. She didn't look at me, but her eyes lingered briefly on Joe. 'What are you doing here?'

'I've come to take you both to Wild World,' said Dad. 'I've had an interesting call about some work for Wild about Animals.'

I brightened. 'We're back in business?'

'Maybe,' Dad smiled. 'A film producer is after some swimming monkeys for a TV link.'

'What's a TV link?' Tori asked.

Joe jumped in before Dad could open his mouth. 'It's those bits that join TV programmes together!'

'Like the HD one with dogs turning into wolves and that,' Cazza added unexpectedly.

We didn't have an HD telly so Cazza's explanation made no sense at all. Before the fire, we'd just had one of those ancient boxes that practically needed winding up every time you watched it.

'I'll have to take your word for that,' said Dad, looking curiously at Cazza. 'Anyway, I'm having a meeting with Matt about it this afternoon. Mum's meeting us up there.'

'Cool,' said Tori.

Cool? My sister *never* said cool. Had the real Tori been kidnapped and replaced by someone who said 'cool' and made friends with the Cazzas of this world and totally ignored her identical twin sister and best mate since the age of thirteen minutes?

'This is Cazza by the way, Dad,' said Tori. She still hadn't registered my presence.

''Lo,' said Cazza with a little toss of her jet-black hair.

'Good to meet you, Cazza,' said Dad. He started to usher me and Tori away. 'Sorry to rush you, girls, but we have to go. I've parked the van in a dodgy spot . . .'

'Can Cazza come to Wild World with us?' Tori said.

Uh-oh.

'Can I come too?' Joe said hopefully.

Two can play at this game, I thought.

'Of course you can.'

I grabbed Joe firmly by the arm and glared at my sister. She glared back. Cazza stood between us, her hands deep in the pockets of her black puffa jacket.

'Right,' said Dad. He scratched his head. 'Don't your, er, parents need to know?'

Cazza produced a gorgeous shiny little black phone from her pocket and waved it casually. I gave a silent moan of envy. Mum and Dad refused to buy us phones.

'My dad's never home before seven,' said Joe in excitement as Dad looked in his direction. 'And it's only three o'clock now. So I can do what I want for four hours!'

Dad looked like he was struggling with a decision. 'Well, that's sorted then,' he said at last. 'Car's round the corner in Abbey Road. Come on. Matt's waiting.'

6

More Serious Than I Thought

It was a weird journey. Tori and Cazza weren't talking to each other, but I think that was because they were comfortable being quiet and not because they hated each other's guts. I was quiet with Tori because just now I *did* hate her guts, and Cazza scared me, frankly. Joe sat like an overwhelmed rabbit in between us, like he couldn't believe he was going somewhere that wasn't straight home to his computer and his Warhammer figures.

It was Cazza who spoke first.

'Sorry about the fire and that.'

'Thanks,' said Dad from the front. 'We are too.'

He swung the van round the corner and on to the main road that would take us to Wild World. I was

38

pleased that we weren't taking the other route past our ruined house.

'Cazza had a fire when she was seven,' said Tori.

'Really?' I stared at Cazza, forgetting for a minute that I was scared of her.

'She lost her hamster,' said Tori.

'That's awful!' I said, horrified.

'I'd like a hamster,' said Joe. It gave me a bit of a shock to hear him speak. For a moment I'd forgotten he was in the van with us.

'Did you lose a lot of stuff, Caz?' I didn't want to do a Zoe and blast Cazza with unwanted questions, but I had to know.

'It was the garage,' said Cazza with a shrug. 'So it was mainly lawnmowers and the barbecue. And Dad's new Range Rover. And Rambo.'

Rambo was clearly the hamster.

'I'm really, really sorry,' I said with feeling.

'Whatever,' said Cazza. 'It was like, five years ago now.'

I adjusted my brain to this new Cazza with a frazzled hamster and the shared experience of a house fire. Now I knew what Tori and Cazza had been talking about so intently at registration. Before I could stop it, a little rush of pleasure ran through my body. I felt guilty at once. It's probably bad to feel pleased about having a tragedy in common with someone, even if they are a person you've been desperate to be mates with since for ever.

We'd reached Wild World. Joe sat forward on his chair, as perky as a meerkat as Dad swung in towards the gates. 'Is this it?' he said a bit unnecessarily. 'Are we here? Do you have to pay to get in?'

Charlie-on-the-gate saw it was Dad and waved us off to the side through a gate marked *Private*.

'Wow!' said Joe as Dad motored up the service road towards Matt's office. 'The private entrance! Cool or what? It's like this place is your very own safari park!'

For a moment I indulged in the glorious thought that we owned Wild World and lived here every day. We'd walk Rabbit past the fields of zebras, and see the lions and tigers every morning before breakfast. We'd get discounts in the shop on the stuffed animal toys, and we'd help ourselves to the pastries behind the counter in the café. And we'd get to go in all the enclosures and make friends with the most incredible animals and get to stroke them and *everything*. What would a rhino's hide feel like? Were red pandas soft or bristly?

'Yeah,' I said dreamily. 'Good, isn't it?'

Mum and Rabbit were waiting for us outside Matt's office. While Joe fussed over Rabbit and Dad shook Matt's hand, I looked over at Tori and Cazza. They were chatting like they'd known each other in a different life or something. I tried to earwig their conversation. If they were still talking about the fire, I could join in.

At first I couldn't make any sense of what they were saying at all.

'Have you noticed how only really sad kids are into the new guy? And those live shows they've started doing – what's that about? He's a Time Lord, not a pantomime dame.'

'Totally . . .'

This was more serious than I thought.

'You OK?' Joe asked, straightening up from petting Rabbit when he clocked my expression.

'She's into *Doctor Who*,' I said urgently out of the side of my mouth.

Joe looked delighted. 'So am I!'

An awful image of Tori, Cazza *and* Joe all laughing at *Doctor Who* jokes in the canteen while I sat on a table all by myself rose like a zombie from a coffin.

'Are you coming in, girls?' Dad said, pausing at the door. 'All spectators and suggestions welcome.'

Tori was too engrossed in her conversation with Cazza to look round.

Joe was still wittering on. 'I think I like the new Doctor best. I mean, that show they did at the Albert Hall was totally amazing, the way—'

'I'd keep that to yourself if I were you,' I said in a low voice, towing him into Matt's office after Mum and Dad.

'Swimming monkeys?' said Matt in surprise as the meeting got underway.

Dad nodded. 'Any suggestions would be great, Matt. As you know, things are . . . difficult for us at the moment.'

I saw Mum squeeze Dad's hand. Matt nodded sympathetically.

'It's going to be hard to keep the business going from the back of our old van until we find somewhere permanent to live, but we don't have much choice,' Dad went on. 'We can't afford to turn work down, however hard the animals might be to find. Since we have such a good relationship with Wild World, we thought we'd ask you first.'

'I didn't know monkeys *could* swim,' Joe whispered to me at the back of the office.

'Depends on the species.' I hadn't grown up in a mad animal house for nothing. 'Some monkeys hate water, others love it. In Japan there are these macaques who take long baths in the hot springs. They are *well* hilarious, aren't they . . .' I remembered Tori was still sitting outside talking to Cazza. 'Anyway, they're well hilarious,' I finished lamely.

'And the film company wants real monkeys instead of CGI ones because . . . ?' Matt checked.

'They'll digitally manipulate the finished product,' Dad explained. 'But they need real swimming monkeys to start with. Any ideas?'

'Proboscis monkeys would be the best,' said Matt, his cheerful face collapsing into a frown as he thought. 'They're great natural swimmers. Trouble is, Wild World doesn't have any. And don't tell me – you're in a hurry?'

'When aren't film companies in a hurry?' Dad said with a sigh. 'I understand if this is impossible, Matt, but any help you can offer would be great.'

7

Barbed Wire in Bare Feet

It was dark when we came out again, Mum and Dad and Matt having moved on from swimming monkeys to arrangements for the cubs to go to their new homes. That's winter for you. Darkness sneaks up like a big black blanket when you're not looking.

Tori and Cazza were still sitting outside on the wall, swinging their legs and chatting.

'You must both be frozen,' said Mum, shivering inside her own jacket.

Tori and Cazza jumped down from the wall and gave identical shrugs, humping their left shoulders into the air and down again in a display of synchronized 'whatever'. The panic I was feeling went up another notch.

'We'll get a bite to eat at the café,' said Dad.

'Cheers, Mr Wild,' said Cazza.

'Yeah, thanks!' Joe added enthusiastically.

Joe looked so happy to be there that you'd be forgiven for thinking he'd been bottle-feeding a baby giraffe, not sitting in a zookeeper's office for forty minutes among boxes of animal feed supplements. Tori and Cazza ran alongside Dad in the direction of the café, laughing about something. Joe took Rabbit's lead and rushed after them.

'What's up?' said Mum, linking arms with me as I trailed at the rear.

'You'd think I understood my twin sister, wouldn't you, Mum?' I muttered. 'We've been practically stuck together at the hip for eleven years. But I don't understand her at all since the fire. Not one bit.'

'And you don't like her new friend much, right?'

Mum had an unnerving ability to read my mind that was almost as bad as Tori's. It's probably because she and I are peas in a pod about most things.

'She's OK,' I said. I decided not to explain about how long I'd tried to befriend Cazza myself. 'I mean, she's kind of scary and she's had more detentions than anyone I've ever met, but she's cool.'

Mum looked alarmed. 'I'm not sure I want Tori

making friends with someone like that,' she said, staring after Tori and Cazza as they ran through the dark trees ahead of us.

'No, seriously, she's fine!' I said hastily. If things weren't bad enough with Tor already, Mum forbidding Tori from seeing Cazza because of something I said would ice the biscuit for sure. 'It's just . . .' It would sound really wet, me being funny about Tori making friends with someone that wasn't me, so I bottled it. 'I don't know,' I finished in a vague kind of way, and hoped Mum wouldn't ask any more questions.

We passed the trees in the new chimpanzee enclosure. Yells of laughter drifted towards us. I guessed Tori and Cazza were chasing each other around the concrete bollards outside the café, because Tor and I did it every time we came to Wild World.

'How long till the rest of the chimps get here, Mum?' I asked, staring up into the dark trees overhead. 'You know, the pregnant female and the others?'

'They're coming on Friday,' said Mum.

'Cool.'

And it was. But it was weird, having to feel happy about it all by myself.

On Friday morning, I stood in the McGuigans' hall

46

and pulled on my coat as fast as was polite.

'Thanks for having me again, Mr McGuigan, Mrs McGuigan,' I said.

'So you're spending the weekend with your grandparents, are you?' said Mr McGuigan jovially. He jingled the keys to his big blue Volvo in one beefy hand. 'Excellent. They'll be pleased to see you. They probably don't have the pleasure very often, being up in Liverpool, eh?'

'It's been wicked having you!' said Zoe, wriggling into her nice, dark-purple All Hallows blazer. 'I'm really glad your house burned down, Taya!'

Wednesday night with the McGuigans had been OK, but last night had been like tightrope-walking on barbed wire in bare feet. Tori had spent the night at Cazza's house. It had been my first night without her, ever. She hadn't even rung me for a bedtime chat. I never knew twelve hours could be so long.

I walked down the McGuigans' front path with my bag slung over my shoulder and hurried along the road to the bus stop. As I'm naturally a chatty person, I kept starting conversations because I forgot Tori wasn't walking next to me. The conversations I kept starting were all angry ones too, which must have made me look like even more of a nutter than if

I'd just been smiling at an imaginary friend.

I glared out of the window when Cazza and Tori got on the bus. It's amazing how interesting a *No Smoking* sticker on a window can be when you know you can't look round. When I judged it was safe to turn back, I cursed myself. Tori was gazing directly at me from underneath Cazza's arm where Cazza had grabbed the holding post.

'All right?' I said gruffly, because I couldn't not say anything.

I saw something scoot across her face like one of those speedy lizards you see on sunny walls in Spain. 'You know,' she said. 'You?'

'You know,' I said back.

It wasn't the most interesting conversation in the world. But I wasn't giving her any more than I had to. *She* was the one who had to start talking to *me* round here.

For a minute, I thought Tori was going to say something else. My heart lifted a little. Then Cazza reached down and whispered something in her ear that made her laugh, and the moment was gone.

'So the new chimps are coming today?' said Joe on my other side.

'Yes,' I said, glad of the distraction. 'The lorry that's

bringing them is coming to Wild World at ten o'clock. The female's due to give birth in a fortnight, so I hope they can settle her in and get her comfortable so she doesn't get too stressed before the baby comes.'

Despite my bad night and morning, I felt a shiver of anticipation in my stomach. Baby chimpanzees were utterly adorable.

'I can't believe there'll be a baby chimp at Wild World soon,' said Tori's voice from the other side of the bus.

I felt a volcanic rush of annoyance. Who did she think she was, butting in like nothing was wrong? She'd ignored me for *two* days.

'Who invited you to join our conversation, Tori?' I snapped.

Tori flushed.

'Chill, Taya,' said Cazza in a bored voice, swinging from her holding pole like some kind of black-haired, badge-wearing, sister-stealing gibbon.

Talk about red rag to a bull. I could feel my face flooding with colour.

'Don't tell me to chill, Cazza,' I hissed. 'This is between me and my sister, all right?'

A little chorus of 'Ooh!'s rippled down the bus.

'Taya,' Tori began. 'Listen—'

'No!'

I felt tall. I felt magnificent. I felt totally and completely furious. All my grief about the fire and all my misery about missing my sister and all my exhaustion about coping with Zoe McGuigan and her stupid, stupid questions by myself last night boiled over like a cauldron of oil.

'I'm not listening to you. I don't know why you're acting like this, Tori, but I'm really sorry we're related just now.'

Tori gave a funny little gasp, lifting her hand to her throat. We stared at each other like two mesmerized snakes. Then the bus broke the spell with that loud farty wheeze it always gives before it stops at the school gates.

'Time to get off,' Joe said awkwardly.

I didn't need telling twice.

8

Picking Up the Pieces

'What kind of message?' asked Joe, hurrying after me at the end of school. 'A message about the chimps?'

'Just a message to say get to Wild World by ourselves,' I said. 'I guess you can come if you want. Oh – you've got chess club, haven't you?'

'Chess club was cancelled so I've got loads of time to kill before Dad gets home,' said Joe. 'But I thought you were going to your grandparents this weekend?'

Our trip to stay with Dad's parents had totally gone out of my head. 'Yeah . . .' I said, briefly flummoxed. 'So did I.'

Now I came to think of it, the message I'd got from the school office *was* a bit weird. Normally when we went to visit Dad's parents, Dad came to school with the van all packed up and ready to go. I wondered if now that we didn't have anything *to* pack, the rules had somehow changed.

'I guess Mum and Dad know what they're doing,' I said doubtfully. 'We've just got to get to Wild World as soon as we can.'

I glanced around automatically for Tori. Then I remembered how I was still mad with her – plus I'd hardly seen her all day because she'd been with Cazza – and I stopped looking. 'As soon as *I* can,' I corrected myself, seeing the bus we needed chugging into view. 'Tori can make her own blinking way there. You coming or what?'

The bus was a single-decker, and not very full. We bagged seats at the back.

'It must be because of the chimps,' said Joe in excitement. 'Don't you think?'

'Mum doesn't have anything to do with the chimps,' I reminded him. 'It's not like she's fostering them or anything. I guess they just need to do a couple of things with the cubs before we head up to Liverpool. That's all.'

How wrong I was.

The bus didn't half go round the houses. It was

practically dark when we got to Wild World.

'Hey, Tori and friend!' said Charlie-on-the-gate in a cheery voice as Joe and I walked over from the bus stop on the other side of the road.

Charlie was a nice enough guy, but I hated how he always mixed me up with my sister – especially just at that moment. 'I'm *Taya*,' I said. 'Charlie, I've been coming to Wild World since I was a toddler and you still don't know the difference between me and her?'

Charlie's freckles all joined up when he smiled. 'Showing your boyfriend the sights?' he teased, making Joe blush to the roots of his sandy-blond hair.

'He's not my boyfriend,' I said through gritted teeth. 'Can we go through?'

'Bit crazy back there,' Charlie called after us as we pushed through the staff gate. 'A transport lorry carrying some new animals crashed on the way down this morning. We're picking up the pieces.'

The blood drained from my face. 'A crash?' I said, spinning round and almost knocking Joe off his feet. 'Not the chimps?'

Charlie looked astonished. 'How did you know that?'

I was already running. I could hear Joe's questions as he tried to keep up – wave upon wave of them – but concentrated on getting to the park office as fast as my legs would let me. Horrifying visions of dead chimpanzees lying pathetically on the side of a busy road surged through my brain as I charged past the ape-house and through the trees.

I burst into Matt's office. 'Are the chimps OK?'

Matt was on the phone. On closer inspection, he was on two: his mobile and the landline, the landline clamped to his chest.

'I'm a bit busy in here, Taya,' he said, putting the mobile next to the landline phone on his chest and looking shattered. 'Your mum's up at the surgery. She'll explain everything.'

'Are they dead?' I asked, feeling hysterical. Joe bobbed around behind me like a worried duck on a stormy sea. It wasn't fair. First a lab, then a car crash? What had the poor chimps done to deserve such bad luck?

Matt waved his hand imploringly at me to go away and lifted one of the phones to his ear again. I flew back out of the office with only one thought in my head: *find Mum*.

The lights were blazing in the modern surgery building towards the back of the park when Joe and I charged up. Joe collapsed against the glass double doors marked *CLOSED TO THE PUBLIC* while he tried to catch his breath. Leaving him there, I stumbled into the reception area. I'd been here a few times before with Mum when she'd been called out to assist with animal emergencies during the holidays.

'Taya!' exclaimed Mary, the lady on the reception. 'It is Taya, isn't it?' she checked a little uncertainly. 'It's awfully hard to tell the difference between you girls.'

We didn't come over to this end of the park very often, so I cut Mary a little more slack than Charlie-on-the-gate. I nodded, too puffed to speak.

'Your mother told me to expect you.' Mary glanced through the glass double doors, clearly expecting Tori to be bringing up the rear.

'Are the chimpanzees dead?' I asked, determined to get an answer from *someone* before I exploded.

Looking back at me, Mary's eyes softened. 'Sadly, we lost one of the males and the pregnant female. Dr Nik did his best, but—'

Dr Nikolaides was the Wild World vet. He was a big Greek guy whose large hairy hands didn't fit with the gentle care he gave to even the smallest animals in the park.

'No!' I wailed.

'They saved the baby,' said Mary, getting up from her desk and coming round to give me a big soap-smelling hug, 'but there was nothing they could do for the mother. It's a tragedy, really it is.'

Part of me registered that this was a bit of good news at least. The rest of me burst into tears for the poor lost female and the poor motherless baby.

The doors leading into the surgery itself swung open. Mum came in, wearing a set of Wild World overalls that was about three sizes too big, her arms full of bottles.

'Mum!' I cried, pulling away from Mary. 'I came as soon as I could, Joe's outside, it's awful! What happened? Is the baby chimp OK? Did the mum give birth at the crash site and then die or did they operate on the mother here and save the baby that way? What—'

'Taya, darling, slow down,' said Mum. She looked exhausted. 'Your dad will explain . . .' She glanced around the reception. 'Where is he, anyway?' she said, sounding tetchy. 'I told him to stay here and wait for you. And where's Tori?'

'I don't know,' I said, desperate to return to the question of the chimps. 'What *happened*, Mum?'

'The transport lorry had a puncture at seventy miles an hour.' Mum's voice broke in the middle, then steadied again. 'The driver swerved, but there was nothing he could do. It was no one's fault. The side of the lorry hit the central reservation . . .'

I rubbed Mum's arm wordlessly. I could see how hard she was trying to keep back the tears.

'The motorway was blocked for three hours while they got a medical team there. The driver and one of the male chimps were shocked but unhurt. The others . . . The second male was dead at the scene; the female was badly injured but still breathing. They got her back here in record time, but it wasn't enough . . .'

'Anita!' came Dr Nik's deep voice from behind a second door. 'Have you got the bottles?'

'I have to go,' said Mum. She shifted the bottles over to the crook of one arm and wiped the tears from my face with her free hand. 'Matt has asked me to help with the little one. He is small and in need of intensive care, but provided we are vigilant he will be fine. It was a miracle, how he was saved . . .'

I pictured the tiny, premature baby chimpanzee somewhere behind those doors, lying on a table with bright lights shining on his lonely little body as the vets tried to save his life.

'When did his mother die?' I asked, almost too choked to speak.

Mum wiped her own eyes. 'About half an hour ago.'

9

The University of Wisdomness

Joe and I sat silently in the reception bit of the surgery, waiting for Dad and Tori to turn up.

'This must be pretty boring for you,' I said to Joe in a dull voice.

Joe lifted up a book. 'I've got chess techniques to read about,' he said.

'Whoopee doo.'

Joe put his book awkwardly back inside his bag and sat with his arms folded across the top of it. The way he acted with that bag often made me wonder if he carried the crown jewels around in it all day long.

'Sorry,' I muttered after a moment. 'I didn't mean to be nasty about it.'

'That's OK.'

The outside doors swung open. Dad was just tucking his phone into the inside pocket of his jacket.

'Sorry, guys,' he said. 'That call went on longer than I expected. Have you been waiting long? Where's—'

'I don't *know* where Tori is,' I said, fed up with that particular question. 'Why should I always know what my stupid sister is doing?'

Right on cue, Tori pushed through the doors. She was out of breath, and her cheeks were flushed rosy with the cold and something that looked like anger.

'Thanks for waiting for your *stupid sister* at school, Taya,' she said coolly.

The little bit of me that felt ashamed for not waiting flared into life like a match. Despite myself, I felt bad. Had it been really horrible not to have waited for her like normal?

I blew the match out. 'What's the matter?' I challenged. 'Cazza didn't walk you safely past Dwight Dingle today? How did that feel, being all by yourself?'

Tori looked at me like I was a slimy worm. 'Aren't we going to Liverpool?' she asked Dad, turning her back on me. 'Why are we at the surgery?'

Dad began to explain when his coat pocket started ringing. He fished his phone out and looked at it.

'Better take this,' he said, looking distracted. 'Taya, tell Tori what happened.'

Tori reluctantly turned back to face me again as Dad disappeared with the phone clamped to his ear.

OK, I thought. *Let's see how long this takes.*

I stared at her without speaking. She stared back. No one blinked. No one breathed. The silence stretched like a rubber band on the verge of twanging and really, *really* hurting someone on the nose.

'I don't have to put up with this,' said Tori at last.

'No,' I agreed. 'You don't. You can catch the bus out of here and go and stay with your new best friend again tonight. A few dead chimpanzees needn't spoil your evening.'

I knew it was harsh the minute I said it, but I couldn't exactly take it back.

Tori paled. 'They died? How?'

'They crashed on the way here,' said Joe.

Tori fell on the chair beside Joe and put her face in her hands. I listened for the sound of tears, but didn't hear anything. That was the thing with Tori. She never cried. *Except after the fire*, my inner voice reminded me.

A nuggety thought came into my head. Was that was this was about? Knowing my sister like I did, her outburst on the common had probably freaked her out as much as me.

A burst of mercy switched on my fingers and made them touch my sister on the shoulder. I waited for her to shrug me off, but she didn't.

'I'm sorry, Taya,' Tori said, her voice muffled by her fingers. 'I'm sorry for cutting you dead and I'm sorry about the chimps but most of all I'm sorry you hate me.'

'I don't hate you,' I said truthfully.

Joe tried to blend in with the seat and hide his face in his chess book as Tori looked up at me, her lips all white as she pressed them together with the effort of not crying.

'It's OK to cry,' I said. 'I've been weeping buckets. So's Mum.'

'What's the point of crying?' she said in a fierce sort of voice. 'It muddles your thinking and makes you look like a prat.'

'Did you feel like a prat at the fire?' I asked curiously.

Tori flushed like a beetroot. 'Don't mention the fire.'

'I will mention it because it's the start of everything,' I said, realizing how true this was the second I said it. 'Reacting like that was OK, Tor. If you don't accept that, you'll just go sour like old milk or bad cheese.

Like, you know when Mum sometimes forgets to take the wet clothes out of the washing machine and you open the door and it stinks? If the clothes had just come out and been hung on the line the minute they were finished – provided it wasn't raining, of course – they would have smelled all lovely and fresh.'

Where was all this wisdom coming from? If I didn't stop talking soon, I was going to get some kind of wisdom award from the University of Wisdomness.

Tori's mouth twitched. 'Are you telling me I smell?'

'Yeah,' I said. 'You totally reek.'

We both started giggling. Maybe it was the shock of the chimps dying, or the relief of being mates again. Whatever it was, it felt really good.

Dad appeared back in the doorway. Still grinning, Tori and I looked at him.

'Found any swimming monkeys yet?' I said, guessing that was what the call had been about.

Dad shook his head. He was looking tired, his skin tinged with grey.

'Your insulin, Dad!' Tori said suddenly. 'Have you taken it today?'

It was really important that Dad kept taking his insulin injections to stop the diabetes from knocking him out. After the week we'd had, Dad putting himself in hospital again was the last thing we needed.

'I'm due to take it,' Dad admitted. 'I'll do it in a minute. Do you think your mother's going to be much longer?'

He checked the surgery doors for any sign that Mum was coming out. They stayed shut.

'I think Mum's going to be here all night,' I said, thinking about the newborn chimp in Mum's soft, calm hands.

'I think so too,' Dad said glumly. 'Sorry, girls, but it doesn't look like we'll make it up to Liverpool this weekend after all.'

'We guessed,' said Tori.

Dad took out his phone again. 'I'll just call the McGuigans to see if they mind—'

'No!' Tori and I both said in horror. It was the *weekend*. Surely we deserved a break from Zoe McGuigan?

'Tori and Taya can stay with me tonight if they want,' said Joe impulsively. 'I'm sure Dad won't mind.'

'Excellent idea!' I said.

'Perfect!' said Tori.

Dad looked puzzled, but dialled Mr Morton's number instead.

'Cheers, Joe,' I said in a low voice.

'Yeah,' said Tori. 'You just saved us from a fate worse than death.'

As she grinned at me, I felt a wash of wonderful relief. My twin was back beside me, where she was supposed to be. Everything was normal again. She hadn't replaced me with Cazza! How stupid was I to have thought she'd do that?

'Maybe we can all do something tomorrow morning!' said Joe eagerly. 'We could go bowling. Or—'

'Sorry, Joe,' said Tori. She shot me an awkward look. 'Cazza asked me to go swimming with her at the Kingfisher Centre. I mean, I told her we were going to Liverpool so I couldn't. But now we're staying – I think I'll probably do that.'

10

Helium Balloon

You've never seen a house as neat as Joe Morton's. I suppose with only Joe and his dad living there, mess just doesn't happen. Especially as Joe's at school all day and his dad's never around.

'Have you got a housekeeping fairy or something, Joe?' Tori said, gazing at the immaculate cream-coloured rug and the beige walls hung with neatly arranged black-and-white photos of motor-racing cars. 'This place is so clean I can almost see my face in the carpet.'

'We've got Magda who comes three times a week,' said Joe. 'But she's not a fairy.'

Tori fixed Joe with one of her unblinking stares. 'Are you sure about that?'

'Pretty sure,' said Joe earnestly. 'She hasn't got wings or anything.'

Tori grinned at me – trying to bring me in on the joke, I guess. I gave her half a smile back. I was still reeling with the knowledge that my twin wanted to spend tomorrow with Cazza Turnbull and not with me. And *swimming*? We never went swimming. I couldn't swim at all, although Tori had her fifty-metre badge. Was she completely mad?

'Can I use your phone, Joe?' Tori asked, putting her bag by the front door. 'To tell Cazza I can meet her at the Kingfisher Centre after all?'

Joe pulled a swanky black banana-shaped stick from some kind of base on the hall table and waved it at Tori.

'Whoa,' said Tori. 'I only want to phone Cazza, not beam myself up to the Starship *Enterprise*.'

While Joe showed Tori what all the buttons on the amazing phone did, I walked into the big black-and-white kitchen and tried my very best to find something to do that meant I wouldn't be listening to Tori's phone call.

'Juice?' said Joe, heading into the kitchen behind me and reaching for the world's most gigantic steel fridge. 'Coke? Milk?'

'*Hi, can I speak to Cazza, please?*'

'Juice!' I said very loudly. 'I love juice. It's so juicy. Mmm, juicy juicy!'

Joe looked a bit surprised but got some juice out.

'*Hiya! Yeah, we didn't go . . .*'

I pressed the button on the big telly that stood on the perfect black granite worktops. Nothing happened. 'Got any crisps?' I said in desperation. 'Lovely crunchy crisps in a lovely crinkly bag?'

'*. . . crashed, yeah. The mother died, which is awful. But the baby survived. Mum's . . .*'

Joe pulled open a long cupboard that made this amazing flick-flack noise as all these shelves swung outwards, displaying crisps and a lot of packet sauces. 'Salt and vinegar? Barbecue beef? Cheesy Wotsits?'

'*My pocket money should cover it, no problem. Could you lend me a cozzie? The fire . . .*'

'Anything!' I practically hollered, galloping over and snatching a bag. 'I'm not fussy.'

'*. . . See you then, yeah? Don't drop the banana!*'

'It's a quote! They're quoting the Doctor at each other!' I said in despair, giving up on making loads of noise with my crisps as I heard my sister enjoying her twin-free life with one of her special proper amused laughs. I sank down on a funky steel kitchen chair, briefly wondering if the mesh would leave a weird pattern on my legs. 'Oh wombats, Joe. What am I going to do?'

We heard the phone slotting back into its base. Tori came into the kitchen.

I wiped the desperate expression off my face and stuck on a big shiny smile instead. 'Salt and vinegar?' I said brightly, holding out my crisps.

'They're Quavers, Taya,' said Tori. 'Why are you smiling at me like a loon?'

I smiled even harder. 'What's wrong with smiling at you?'

'You're scaring me,' said Tori. 'It's only swimming,' she added. 'You're not worried about it, are you?'

It was hard keeping a smile up at that level, to be honest. 'Very perspiration of you,' I muttered, deciding it was pointless to deny it.

'The word's *perspicacious*, you wonk,' said Tori, grinning.

'Hello?' I demanded, yanked out of my panic and planted firmly in the mad-with-Tori bit of my brain garden. 'I thought this was the weekend, not an English lesson.'

'Why don't you come too?' Tori suggested. 'Cazza won't mind. That's if you've got enough pocket money left over since your last splurge in Claire's Accessories?'

'No thanks,' I said. 'I don't fancy being a gooseberry.' A sinking gooseberry at that, I added silently to myself. Besides, Claire's Accessories *had* totally cleaned me out. And to add insult to injury, all the stuff I'd bought had gone up in flames.

The phone in the hall gave a tinkling little ring like an electronic waterfall. Joe answered, then handed it to me.

'Hello, Taya darling,' Mum said on the other end. 'I thought I would call and check that everything is OK.'

Nothing was OK. Our house was gone, blameless animals were dead and my twin was drifting away from me like an autumn leaf.

'We're fine, Mum,' I said, holding the phone gingerly in case I pressed a button that would summon helicopters by mistake. 'How's the baby chimp?'

'So far so good, but he needs twenty-four-hour attention. How's Dad?'

'A bit quiet,' I said, remembering how Dad was when he dropped us off. 'He misses you already.'

Mum laughed in a tired sort of way. 'This has only just begun! I hope he can cope by himself for a little while longer. Listen, Taya. I want you and Tori to think of a name for the little chimp and tell me tomorrow, yes?'

I cheered up a little. Naming our animals was always really good fun. 'Tori's going swimming with Cazza tomorrow morning,' I said.

'If that's OK?' Tori called into the receiver over my shoulder.

A little bit of me wanted Mum to say that it *wasn't* OK and Tori couldn't go and she wanted us both up at Wild World first thing.

'That's good,' said Mum. 'I'm glad Tori has a new friend. And you must be glad too, Taya darling.' I squeezed the phone hurriedly to my ear, hoping Tori hadn't heard that part. 'You and Joe can come over together in the morning, and Tori can come later.'

I knew Mum was right. I had to try and be OK about Tori and Cazza. It was going to be hard. You know that major life lesson about loving someone enough to let them go? I did it with a helium balloon once. Biggest mistake of my life.

'How's the little chimpanzee?' Tori asked as I replaced the receiver thoughtfully.

'He's doing really well,' I said. 'Mum says we should think of a name for him.'

'How about Maliketh?' said Joe in excitement. 'Or Shadowblade? No – Grimnir!'

'This is a chimpanzee we're talking about, not a dragon,' I said.

We trailed into the super-clean living room, arguing about names.

'Big Ears!'

'That is the most rubbish name I've ever heard. Dalek?'

'No *way*!'

'Gandalf.'

'Joe! Per*lease*!'

'How about Grandpa?' said Tori.

I stopped punching Joe on the arm. 'What?'

'We didn't see Grandpa this weekend,' said Tori. 'So maybe it's kind of appropriate.'

'And chimps do look like wrinkly old men,' Joe added.

Grandpa was cute. Nearly as funny as Rabbit the dog. I couldn't help giggling as I pictured the confusion that could arise.

'I love it!' I said.

Don't go thinking I was smarming up to Tori just because I was scared of losing her to Cazza. It really was a great name.

11

A Zebra Doing Breaststroke

'Oh!' I breathed in wonder. 'Can I touch him?'

Grandpa was fast asleep in Mum's arms, like a cross between a really old man and a very wrinkly baby, with the most enormous pair of pale pinky-brown ears. He had a weeny nappy on and a tiny woolly hat keeping his head warm, even though the ape-house was already pretty toasty. Dr Nik stood beside Mum, smiling. They looked like a pair of proud parents showing off their baby for the first time. Dad stood to the side, fiddling with his phone.

'He may have been born early and in terrible circumstances, but he is a good weight,' Mum said. I stroked Grandpa's warm cheek. 'And he has taken to the bottle-feeding very well.'

Grandpa chose that moment to yawn. His cute factor rocketed into the stratosphere. Joe stretched out his hands and then snatched them back again, like he didn't quite trust himself not to hug Grandpa to death.

The other chimps – the male and female who'd arrived first, and the male that had escaped the crash unhurt – all watched Grandpa from their glass-walled enclosure, which looked in on the atrium where we were all standing. The female looked particularly interested, stretching up on her back legs and pressing her leathery palms against the glass.

'I think the other chimps want to meet him,' Joe said.

'They already have,' said Dr Nik in his deep, accented voice. 'We've introduced everyone through the glass. We'll show them Grandpa every day so they all get used to each other. Hopefully we can get him in there very soon. I have high hopes that the female will adopt him. She seems very interested.'

Dad had a funny look on his face as Mum smiled at Dr Nik and nuzzled Grandpa. Grandpa opened his clear hazel-green eyes, stretched out two skinny black arms and clutched at her shirt. Then – and I am not kidding – he started sucking his thumb.

'He's so *human*!' I said.

'He's also hungry,' said Mum as Grandpa sucked hard on his thumb and started making little *woomph*ing noises.

'He's bottle-feeding every two hours at the moment,' said Dr Nik. 'Then some cuddles and a few hours in the incubator so he can sleep and grow. What a life, hey, Grandpa?'

Grandpa showed his little gums in a funny startled expression, then sucked his thumb more noisily than ever.

'Do you want to hold him while your mother does his milk?' Dr Nik asked me as we went into the back room where the food and bottles were kept.

My tummy was full of disco-dancing fairies as I took the hairy little bundle and cradled him carefully. Grandpa's eyes were like shiny brown marbles as he *whoomph*ed away in my arms. Practically the whole of his hand was in his mouth now.

'He's so cute it hurts,' I moaned.

'Magic,' whispered Joe.

'That's just normal baby milk,' I said, pulling myself out of my chimp love swamp as I saw Mum take a box of milk powder off a shelf and prise off the lid. 'Where's the chimpanzee stuff?'

'Human formula is the best thing for orphaned chimps like Grandpa,' said Mum.

Dr Nik stayed with Mum while she mixed up the formula and put it in the microwave. Joe and I had a quick snoop around the rest of the ape-house with Grandpa still cradled in my arms. The ape-house wasn't open to the public yet, and was still really new and full of the smell of drying paint and freshly varnished wood.

'Who's going in this one, Dad?' I said, peering into an empty enclosure beside the chimps.

Dad didn't hear the question. He was on another monkey mission call, pacing around the atrium. Each time he got near the ape-house door, Rabbit thought they were going outside for a walk and her tail went into a frenzy. And then each time Dad turned and paced back again, her tail drooped. It was kind of funny to watch.

'I know I said we'd find some monkeys for you, Graham . . . And we will . . . We've just— Yes, yes, I understand you're in a hurry . . . I'll have an answer for you soon, OK?' He snapped the phone shut, looking harried. 'Did you say something, Taya?'

'What's going to live in here?' I said, shifting Grandpa to the crook of my arms and tapping the glass.

'Long-tailed macaques, Matt said,' Dad answered in a distracted sort of way. 'Coming on Tuesday.'

'Macaques can swim,' Joe piped up. 'I've seen it on YouTube.'

'I saw some swimming when I was on a photography job in Indonesia,' Dad nodded. 'Unfortunately, these macaques were bred in a laboratory and have never seen water in their lives.'

More laboratories. There was something seriously wrong with a world that could fly to the moon and invent something as magical as the internet but still used live animals in labs. Just then I was pretty glad I wasn't a macaque.

'Taya?' said Joe. He was moving his arms up and down, weightlifting with nothing in his desperation to hold Grandpa. 'Can I . . . ? Do you think I can . . . ?'

I glanced over at Dr Nik, who was propping open the back-room door with his massive shoulders. He nodded with a smile.

'Sure,' I said, turning back to Joe. 'Sit down and hold out your arms.'

Joe sat down so fast he practically had a motion blur around him. He took Grandpa like he was receiving an blast of angelic light into his soul.

'Couldn't you teach the macaques, Dad?' I asked

once I was sure Joe was holding Grandpa the right way. 'You taught Tori at the Kingfisher Centre last summer.'

'I might have taught your sister,' Dad said, 'but I wasn't very successful with you, was I?'

If I'm totally honest, I hadn't tried very hard when Dad gave me and Tori swimming lessons. I couldn't get my head around the idea of paddling along in deep places where you couldn't put your feet down. And yes, I panicked when I couldn't touch the bottom of the pool with my toes. And then I sank and swallowed half the pool, which meant I swallowed a whole lot of wee because everyone knows little kids wee in swimming pools.

It had been enough to put me off trying again.

'I think that was my fault, not yours,' I said honestly.

'Nice idea, Taya, but no way,' Dad said.

'What's a nice idea?' said Matt, coming into the ape-house with a bunch of boxes nicely balanced on his jutting tummy. Rabbit sniffed hopefully at the outside air that came blasting in with him.

'Taya thinks her dad could teach the new macaques how to swim,' Joe said. He rocked Grandpa very gently. The tiny chimp grasped his fingers tight.

Matt put down his boxes and looked thoughtful.

'That's not a bad idea,' he said. 'I didn't think of it before. Macaques are natural swimmers in the wild, so it probably wouldn't be difficult to introduce our lab-bred macaques to the water. It would solve two problems at once: your swimming monkeys and our unfit ones. Jonas? What do you think?'

'Good idea,' agreed Dr Nik.

'Where will you teach them?' I asked curiously. I couldn't see the Kingfisher Centre taking in a troupe of macaques somehow.

'We have a hydrotherapy pool we use for injured animals,' said Matt. 'We're one of the only zoos in the country with one. We had a zebra in there just yesterday.'

I pictured a zebra doing breaststroke up and down the Wild World pool with a little pink swimming hat on. Cool!

'But I don't know anything about teaching monkeys to swim!' Dad protested.

'You don't have to,' said Dr Nik. 'Talk to James, our animal physiotherapist, about it. I'll call him and set up a meeting for you if you like.'

'Go on, Dad!' I urged as Dad hesitated. 'Then you can call that Graham guy back with good news!'

Mum came out of the back room to fetch Grandpa

for his feed. Joe handed over the little chimp reluctantly and Mum dashed off again, closely followed by Dr Nik.

'Well,' Dad said at last, his eyes following Mum and Dr Nik through the swinging back-room door. 'I've got nothing to lose, have I? It's not like I'm needed around here.'

I frowned at Dad's tone. Was he jealous of Grandpa?

'And maybe I've got some Wild About Animals work to gain,' Dad went on. 'OK, Matt. We'll give it a go.'

Jo and I high-fived in triumph and I broke into a little monkey dance. You know, just for fun.

'What's the excitement?' said Tori, coming through the double doors into the ape-house.

I stopped dancing at once, in case Cazza was about to pile in behind Tori and see me acting like a nutcase. 'Had fun at the pool?' I said as casually as I could.

'Yes, thanks,' said Tori, putting her bag down on the floor. 'Is this about Grandpa?'

I was glad Joe was there to explain. It was already getting boring having to tell Tori stuff, instead of having her experiencing it at the same time as me.

'Good idea, Taya,' said Tori when Joe had finished

repeating everything. She fussed over Rabbit for a bit, then swung back to Dad. 'Could Cazza come and see a swimming lesson one day?'

Here we go, I thought.

'We haven't fixed anything up yet!' Dad said.

'But I can bring her when it's fixed?' Tori pleaded.

Dad started forward as a door swung open. Dr Nik and Mum came into the atrium, Grandpa in Mum's arms suckling on his bottle.

'Hi, Mum!' said Tori eagerly. 'How's Grandpa?'

'Great,' said Mum. She rubbed Grandpa's tummy gently. The chimp gurgled a bit, then clamped his gums more tightly around the milk teat. 'Come and meet him.'

Tori gently fussed over Grandpa. She has the same stillness as Mum when animals are vulnerable. It's not something I'm so good at. A rubbish swimmer, an overexcited animal carer. It was no wonder Tori was going off me, I thought sadly. Glancing across at Dad, I caught a similar expression on his face as he watched Mum and Dr Nik with Grandpa. It looked like we were both missing our other half.

'She still likes you, you know,' said Joe, making me jump. 'I mean, you're her sister.'

Like *that* meant anything.

'Yeah,' I said, hastily rearranging my face so it didn't look like someone had just died. 'Course she does. Come on, Joe. Let's get something to eat at the café.'

12

Momentary Lapse

It was a funny week. Nights with the McGuigans, days at Forrests, evenings at Wild World and then back to the McGuigans again. Just seeing Mum and Dad and Rabbit in the evenings was starting to feel like visiting time after twenty-one hours of life in two different prisons – especially as Mum was so busy with Grandpa. Dad was suffering almost as much as us, and I'd noticed he'd been quite snippy lately. Poor Rabbit hadn't been getting many walks either.

On top of everything else, it was time to say goodbye to the cubs.

Yellowberry Park and Sandown Safari – Chips and Gravy's new homes – were both great, but they were quite a long way away. It would be months, maybe even years, before we saw our tigers again. Imagine having two pet cats right from kittenhood, and then having to let them go like they never belonged to you in the first place. Pants, right?

'They'll be fine,' Dave, the tiger keeper, assured us on Tuesday afternoon as Dad, Tori and I clustered around the tiger enclosure with faces as long as rakes.

'I guess,' I muttered. 'When are the trucks coming to fetch them?'

'In about fifteen minutes,' said Dave, checking his watch.

'Mum had better get a move on,' Dad said. 'You'd think she'd want to say goodbye. Surely someone else can take Grandpa for a while?'

'She'll be here,' I said, rubbing Dad's arm.

Growling softly, Chips and Gravy were pacing up and down in the fenced-off run beside us, their ears pricked and their whole bodies on alert like they knew something was up. Chips stood up straight, stretching his long paws up the mesh as far as they would go. He was taller than Dad when he did that.

'Bye, Chips,' I whispered. 'Be good.'

'Don't forget us, will you?' Tori added, her voice suddenly sounding choked.

Gravy turned his golden head towards us and

blinked his wonderful wise eyes. '*Vuvuvuv*,' he said.

'That was goodbye,' I sobbed, watching as Rabbit snuffled through the mesh at the cubs. 'Did you hear that? He actually said goodbye!'

'You talk such rubbish, Taya,' said Tori.

'Tori, now isn't the time to get all realistic and boring. Now's the time—'

'It wasn't goodbye, you doughnut,' said my twin, putting her arm round me. 'It was "I love you". Anyone could have told you that.'

We heard the sound of two rumbling trucks coming up the service road.

'The taxi service is early,' said Dave in surprise. 'Andy, do you think Anita's going to—'

Anita came hurrying up the road, just behind the trucks. 'I'm here!' she called, waving at us. 'I'm here!'

'About time,' Dad muttered.

Given everything we were dealing with, it was only a matter of time before Tori and I hit meltdown. And when we did, we did it in style.

'It must be great, just having one single bag of stuff in the whole entire world!' said Zoe on Thursday evening. She smoothed the fluffy cushions on her big soft purple duvet and straightened out the million stuffed rabbits that lined the head of her bed. 'My auntie Sarah thinks we've become too materialistic. She says we could live on just five per cent of the stuff we own and we should all declutter *big* time. You guys are *way* ahead.'

Walking over to Zoe's extensive nail polish collection, Tori wordlessly scooped them into her arms and put them in the bin with a crash. Zoe sat up in alarm.

'What are you doing?'

'Decluttering,' said Tori.

As Zoe gasped and protested, Tori yanked open a window before attacking the wardrobe and gathering a huge armful of clothes. I watched in horrified delight as she flung the clothes outside, where they fluttered down through the darkness and draped themselves over the trampoline below.

'Mum!' Zoe shouted, rushing for the bedroom door. 'Tori's gone mad!'

'Catch,' said Tori, grinning as she flung an armful of Zoe's stuffed rabbits at me.

A giddy kind of madness descended on us. As Zoe screeched for her mum, the rabbits hurtled out of the window in an arc of fluff and shiny glass eyes. Tori and I stripped off the purple duvet cover and matching pillowcase on the bed next. These also went out of the window, floating like multicoloured parachutes in the moonlight.

'What on *earth* is going on?'

Mrs McGuigan stood panting in the doorway, Zoe wailing behind her.

'It was Zoe's idea, Mrs McGuigan,' said Tori, lobbing balled-up pairs of pink socks out into the night – *ping! ping! ping!* – with bull's-eye accuracy. 'She thinks life would be much better without any stuff. So we thought we'd help.'

'Stop!' Mrs McGuigan looked like she was going to collapse. 'Really! I—'

'Not my PJs!' Zoe howled. 'Not my bunnies!'

'Gordon!' Mrs McGuigan screeched, charging up and down the landing like a crazed hedgehog. 'Gordon! Call Anita and Andy *right now*!'

Zoe's dad came thundering up the stairs, his phone in his hand. 'Andy? Andy? Come and get your daughters before they wreck my house!'

The giddiness shooting through me like molten gold started to harden and chill in my veins as I realized the kind of trouble we were in. Tori was still giggling helplessly, a few pairs of Zoe's knickers in one hand and a pencil case in the other.

'Not much time left before we're grounded for ever,'

she said, a mad glint in her eyes. 'Hey, do you think you can be grounded when you haven't got a house to be grounded *in*? I vote we try and chuck Zoe out the window too.'

On Friday morning, Tori and I sat in the green-painted office of Mrs Duvall, the Forrests school councillor. She gazed at us with big sympathetic eyes.

'Of *course* you're upset about your house,' she said in her breathy, hypnotic voice. 'Have you spoken to anyone about it? Have you shared your feelings?'

Privately I thought we'd shared our feelings rather well with the McGuigans. And with Dad too, when he tore strips off us for being so ungrateful to Zoe's family.

Mrs Duvall turned to my sister. 'How about you, Tori?'

Tori had that special look in her eyes that told me she was reciting the entire script of her favourite *Doctor Who* episode in her head. I didn't fancy Mrs Duvall's chances of getting a word out of her.

'It must be very unsettling for you, to have no permanent place to live at the moment,' Mrs Duvall breathed on.

'It's horrible, Mrs Duvall,' I agreed. 'We said sorry to Zoe last night when Dad came to collect us, but she didn't want to listen. Her favourite rabbit had landed in the pond, you see.'

Mrs Duvall scribbled something down in tiny writing on the pad of paper in front of her. *The Wild girls have cracked and gone insane*, I imagined her writing. *Taya is talking nonsense about rabbits and ponds. Tori is so damaged she can't even speak.*

Laying her pen down, Mrs Duvall gazed at us both again. Tori's eyes had closed now, her lips moving very slightly. I guessed she'd reached an exciting part.

'Tell me what happened,' Mrs Duvall said.

'Our house burned down,' I explained.

'But how did it make you *feel*?' Mrs Duvall pressed.

'Horrible,' said Tori suddenly, opening her eyes. 'OK? Completely and totally awful. That's all you need to know really, Mrs Duvall. If you want more words that mean exactly the same thing, I can recommend a thesaurus. May we leave now? We're late for French.'

Mrs Duvall's eyes looked more sympathetic than ever as we shut her door behind us with some relief and hurried off to Mr Jones's class.

'What *is* it about talking?' Tori complained. 'I mean, it's just talk. Hot air. Noise. I wish everyone would just leave us alone. OK, so we trashed Zoe's bedroom, but she was really asking for it. No one died. No one got hurt.'

'Apart from the soggy rabbit,' I agreed.

'We're just *sad*! Why don't people get it?'

'*Assayez-vous, immediatement*,' Mr Jones barked as we came into the French classroom.

Tori sat next to Cazza. Joe was right at the front, wedged in beside the silent Biro. I dropped my bag in the space beside Tori, trying to ignore the ugly stares from Cash 'n' Carrie – Heather Cashman and Carrie Taylor, dire double act and Cazza's so-called mates.

'All right?' Cazza said, flipping a bit of chewing gum around in her mouth. 'I hear you got done for vandalism last night. Nice one.'

'There's nothing nice about ruining someone's stuff,' said Tori, getting out her books. 'It was a momentary lapse, Caz. So you can forget all that "nice one" rubbish.'

I braced myself for a nasty ripping-off-head incident.

'Momentary lapse,' said Cazza, nodding meekly. 'Cool.'

Meekly! How had my sister done this? How had she tamed the monster of Class 7H? It was as if someone had just put a collar and lead on a rabid dog and taught it to beg for biscuits. If I hadn't seen it with my own eyes, I'd never have believed it.

'Oi! Jenkins!' Mr Jones roared at a boy flicking snot at the whiteboard, jolting me out of my thoughts. 'OUT!'

13

Floating Bits of Monkey Poo

Just as Ms Hutson had promised, 'O Christmas Tree' was improving. Although you could say everyone had their own spin on it.

'O Christmas Tree,' sang Jonno Nkobe, drumming on his mate Tosh's head.

'I need a wee,' giggled Cash 'n' Carrie.

'Yo!' sang Cazza whenever there was a suitable pause.

' ,' sang Biro, i.e. he didn't sing anything.

It was a week to go until the concert, and we still hadn't practised it with the steel band or the rest of the Year Sevens. There were going to be nearly three hundred of us all on stage at the same time, which was *crazy*. I knew Ms Hutson's CD by heart now, and wondered if the real band would do it exactly the same or confuse us all with different rhythms.

'Dress rehearsal next week!' called Ms Hutson as the bell went and we all piled off to maths. 'Costumes: red and white, as you all know.'

'Red and white?' said Cazza. 'That is *well* unoriginal.'

'Black isn't a Christmassy colour, Bat Girl,' Tori pointed out.

Cazza was getting better at laughing at herself, I'd noticed. Tori's sarcasm was probably quite refreshing, after having Cash 'n' Carrie agreeing with everything Cazza said and did. I remembered Ms Hutson's funny remark about Tori and Cazza being an interesting combination. I recognized that it was true. They seemed to bring good things out in each other.

'Yes, Biro?' said Ms Hutson behind us.

I twisted round and looked back into the classroom. Silent Biro was asking Ms Hutson something. I couldn't hear what. Maybe he was using sign language.

Rob made his small house stretch a bit bigger and squeezed us in with Mum and Dad after we were chucked out by the McGuigans. It smelled of mice and his sofabed was lumpy, and of course we had to look at the miserable ruins of our old house every day. But at least we were with Mum and Dad and

Rabbit again. Well – Dad and Rabbit anyway. Mum was still spending every second at Wild World with Grandpa.

The macaques arrived on Tuesday, as arranged. Tori and I stood outside their glass enclosure after school on Tuesday afternoon, watching as they carefully checked out their new home. The biggest monkey was the first to try swinging from part of the climbing structure in the enclosure. He did quite well, but fell off after about three swings.

'They'll get the idea,' said Dr Nik, standing behind us with Dad. 'In the wild they spend most of their time in the trees. Lovely creatures, aren't they?'

The macaques weren't as cute as Grandpa, but they had clever inquisitive faces and amazingly flexible tails. They ranged in colour from grey to mid-brown and moved around like lightning. But the bit I liked best about them was the way their fur swept up on top of their heads in a spiky crest, like hairy tree-dwelling punks.

'That one's got a moustache,' said Tori, pointing to the big monkey who'd been first to experiment with swinging about. Sure enough, a snowy-white old soldier-like 'tache jutted out on either side of the monkey's face.

'What, what, old bean,' I said in my best posh army voice.

'We should call him Old Bean,' said Tori.

Dr Nik waved a hand at the other seven macaques. 'Feel free to name them all, girls. How soon do you want these swimming lessons, Andy?'

'Hmph?' Dad had clearly been miles away.

'Swimming lessons, Dad,' I said. 'For the macaques?'

'All right, all right!' said Dad, suddenly all fed up. 'I heard it the first time, thank you, Taya.' He shoved his phone back into his pocket. 'James, the animal physio, thinks the macaques might be ready for some exercise early next week. Where is your hydrotherapy pool anyway, Doctor Nikolaides?'

'Call me Jonas,' said Dr Nik genially. 'It's around the back of Greenings. One of the keeper houses here at Wild World. Near the tigers, you know?'

I pictured the tall chimneys and the laurel hedge. We'd passed Greenings each time we went to visit Chips and Gravy. It looked gorgeous. I envied the keeper who lived there.

'That one should be called Tiny,' said Tori, pointing to the smallest monkey as Matt came in and he, Dad and Dr Nik fell into a conversation about swimming arrangements and film crews.

'And that one's Punk,' I said. 'The one with the really funky crest on his head.'

Tori laughed. 'And can we have one called Dalek?'

'As long as that one there can be Sparkle.'

All we had to do was look at the macaques and the names flowed like water. Dalek was the perfect name for a mean-looking male with one snaggly tooth that made him look like he was permanently snarling. Sparkle was a pretty little female with very bright, busy brown eyes who spent a lot of time preening her fur.

'Maybe we should call her Taya instead of Sparkle,' said Tori.

I stopped plaiting my hair hurriedly and flipped it over my shoulder. 'Shut up, Tor.'

One of the bigger females got named Quango in a genius moment because she was clutching a piece of mango in one of her paws and it rhymed. Specs had these dark rings around her eyes, so her name was pretty obvious. And last of all, we had Fatso.

'Fatso's my favourite,' I said, gazing at the big-bellied monkey crouched in the corner. 'He so looks like he ate all the pies.'

'He's the one who'll benefit the most from his swimming lessons,' said Dr Nik, breaking off his conversation with Matt and Dad.

Old Bean, Tiny, Punk, Dalek, Sparkle, Quango, Specs and Fatso were all scampering like mad about their enclosure now, getting braver in their new environment with every passing minute.

'So are you girls going to watch them learn how to swim?' said Dad. He seemed to have cheered up a bit now that progress was being made.

Tori looked excited. 'Can we go in the pool with them?'

'Macaques are pretty dirty,' said Dr Nik, 'so I wouldn't advise it.'

'But if you want to swim about in water decorated with floating bits of monkey poo . . .' Dad added.

'Gross!' I said as Tori pretended to retch. Swimming with monkeys was a cool idea, but there were limits.

'Can Cazza come?' Tori asked.

I tried not to react, apart from asking: 'And Joe too?'

'No one else, I'm afraid.' Dr Nik sounded apologetic as he patted Rabbit. 'It isn't the Kingfisher Centre.'

'The pool's free on Monday next week,' Dad said. 'We'll do it after school, shall we? We'll have to do it without Mum, though.' And under his breath he added, 'No change there.'

14

Whoops, My Sides Just Exploded

Walking past our old house got a little easier, the more we did it. Tori still refused to look in through the gate. But I felt it was disrespectful to the house and to all the memories we had of living there. So I made myself look. And then I made myself choose a happy memory before I moved on down the road.

'Do you remember the first time Mum brought Fernando home?' I said, running to catch up with Tori as we headed for CostQuik on Saturday morning.

Tori didn't answer.

'I thought he was a new draught excluder for the sitting-room door,' I went on. 'You know they never found their bodies, don't you? Maybe the snakes have taken up on the dodgy bits of Fernleigh Common and are scaring dog-walkers to death these days.'

'Can we not talk about this, Taya?' said Tori, still walking a little way ahead of me. 'You know I hate it. Of course they're dead. I wish you wouldn't try and cheer me up all the time.'

CostQuik was decked out like a Christmas tree. There were so many gold baubles dangling from the polystyrene ceiling that I was practically blinded. Christmas music played jauntily through the speakers up and down the aisles and the staff wore silly Christmas hats.

'I've only just realized,' I said, stopping dead while Tori chose some bagels for breakfast. 'It's Christmas in two weeks.'

'Jingle Bells' sang out madly overhead as Tori negotiated a loop of bright-red tinsel to get to the bagels. 'Really?' she said. 'I hadn't noticed.'

'Whoops, my sides just exploded,' I said witheringly.

Tori put the bagels in her basket. 'Well, the good news is that we've only got one week of school left.'

'Yes, but then what?' I bit the side of my thumb. 'Christmas is going to be extremely weird this year.'

I felt my eyes start to tear up. I was doing quite well about the whole not having a house thing. But Christmas without a house would be like Mum without animal hairs all over her clothes. *All wrong*.

'Hey, maybe we can go to Gran and Pops!' I said, suddenly hitting on the answer. 'They always do wicked Christmases.'

'If we did that, Mum would have to stay here,' Tori pointed out. 'Grandpa can't come to Liverpool. Dad would be in an even filthier mood than he is right now.'

My plan slunk off in defeat. Christmas was sounding worse and worse. No house, no Mum, and Dad in a permanent sulk?

'We've got to make a plan *right now*,' I said, clutching my sister's arm. 'Otherwise Crimbo is going to sneak up on us like a vicious algebra test.'

'I'm going swimming with Cazza this afternoon,' said Tori. 'Besides, I like algebra.'

My sister had a heart of stone. 'This isn't the time for *swimming*!' I said. 'We have to get organized, or we'll end up like those homeless orphans you see in Christmas movies.'

'Come swimming with us,' Tori said.

'I can't swim,' I said through gritted teeth. 'You know that.'

'You should practise.' Tori paid for the bagels and slid them into a bag. 'What if you fall in the hydrotherapy pool during the macaques' swimming lesson? Come on, Taya. It'll be fun.'

'I'd rather do extra geometry,' I said.

To tell the truth, an afternoon in the Kingfisher Centre would be more interesting than an afternoon cooped up on my own in Rob's spare room, trying to block out the smell of mice and watching *The Wizard of Oz* – the only DVD he owned. If I could just avoid drowning, it might be OK.

Tori scooped up her change and headed for the shop door. I scurried after her, running out of excuses a little faster than completely necessary.

'I haven't got a cozzie!'

'The house insurance came through yesterday. Dad'll give us some money. They've got loads at the Kingfisher Centre. Think of it as a shopping trip, Taya.'

My sister knew exactly how to press my buttons.

'Well . . . OK,' I said grudgingly. I couldn't give in too easily, could I? 'Just don't go off and leave me looking like a dork.'

'You don't need any help from me in that department.'

'Tori? You're so sharp you should have a scabbard,' I said.

The cozzies at the Kingfisher Centre were pink, purple, red and bright turquoise with green straps. I loitered for ages at the rack, dreamily imagining myself on a high diving board in the purple one with sparkly crystal straps.

'And here comes Taya Wild. My word, what a fabulous costume! See how the crystals catch the light as she twists and spins and enters the water with hardly a splash!'

'You coming or what?' said Cazza.

Cazza's mum stood to one side, tapping on her BlackBerry, looking like she was in the office even though she was just standing in the leisure centre waiting to keep an eye on us all in the pool. She was dead elegant and even scarier than Cazza.

I hooked the sparkly purple cozzie off the rail, fumbling with the crisp twenty-pound note Dad had given me at lunch. A glossy sheet about swimming lessons sat by the till. I picked one up and stuffed it in my pocket. I can't resist shiny leaflets.

The Kingfisher pool is Fun Central. There are slides and sprinkly fountain things in the shallow end. A couple of water cannons and a sea monster that lurches out of the deep end at you and jets you with water. Steps and paddling pools and a waterfall you could swim underneath. Cool if you can swim. Freaky if you can't.

'I'm going on there.' I pointed at the baby slide and tried to sound breezy about it. 'Anyone coming?'

Cazza looked at me like I had a raccoon tap-dancing on my head. 'See you at the top, Tori,' she said. Adjusting her black swimsuit, she crawled splashily past the sea monster towards the Kingfisher's mega-slide, the Tornado Twister.

'Right,' I giggled, turning to my sister. 'Like you'd ever go . . .'

Tori was already swimming after Cazza. She wasn't going on the Tornado Twister, was she? Even *Dad* wouldn't go on the Tornado Twister. The only people who went on the Tornado Twister were the scary guys who hung around the bus stop near the Carphone Warehouse.

But apparently, Tori was. I watched her climb out of the pool and head up the Tornado Twister steps with Cazza. She didn't even look back to catch my eye and pull an 'Oh my wombats!' kind of face.

Great. I was on my own, watching my sister about to commit suicide. Seeing as there was no *way* I was going to do the same thing, and seeing how I'd paid five pounds seventy to Have Fun, I sat down at the top of the baby slide, stuck on my most nonchalant face and checked out the scene.

I don't know if I'm just weird this way, but I think people all look like different types of animal if you look hard enough. The big lad floating on his back, his belly poking out of the water like a pale strawberry blancmange: hippo. The lady with thin arms doing front crawl up and down the deep end with a green flowery swimming hat and skin like an old brown handbag: alligator. The gaggle of girls in black cozzies shrieking every time the water cannon exploded: blackbirds in a field just when a bird-scarer goes off.

I was just getting into my stride when the baby slide turned slidey. Landing in a clumsy heap at the bottom, I coughed madly and wiped water from my eyes and hoped a) that no one had seen and b) that Tori would get at least twice as much water up *her* nose on the Twister.

Ha! I thought. *She'll never do it. Not for a billion bananas.*

Just as I reached the *bananas* bit of this thought, Tori exploded out the end of the Twister.

'That was your sister?' said a boy's voice above me.

My nose hurt from the water I'd just breathed in at

the shock of seeing my twin fire into the pool like a dart out of a spectacularly huge Nerf gun. Questions raced around my brain like crazed ferrets. Had Tori just drowned? Who was this boy? How did he know my sister? Was my hair dead unflattering and wet in all the wrong places?

'You're Biro!' I said in astonishment, getting my first proper look at the boy who'd spoken.

Biro Lohoni never spoke. Not in maths. Not in English, or science, or registration. Not at lunch. So you can understand my confusion now he'd spoken four whole words at me.

'I didn't know you sounded like that!' I said.

Biro looked a bit like he regretted asking the question about Tori. He had a long face and big brown eyes, a straight nose and floppy black hair that fell in his eyes. *Horse*, I thought.

'It was my sister, yes,' I said, when it became clear he wasn't going to say anything else. 'She's a nutcase, doing that. It's Cazza's fault. Cazza Turnbull. You know her?'

Biro nodded, a little grimly.

'She and Tori are best mates now,' I said, trying not to sound snippy about it. 'Do you swim here a lot then?'

'I can't swim,' Biro said.

'Me neither!' I said.

We smiled at each other, united in our patheticness.

'You lost your house,' Biro said next.

The simple way Biro said this was a million times better than the wide-eyed sympathy of Zoe McGuigan. 'Yes,' I said. 'We did.'

'I lost my house too,' said Biro.

'WHOOO!' screeched Cazza as she hurtled out of the Twister. She did this ungainly roly-poly thing and hit the water face-on, arms and legs whirling. She looked like Incy Wincy Spider having a bad day on the water spout.

'Ouch,' I said.

Biro snorted. I looked at him in surprise. And before you knew it, we were both laughing like a pair of maniacs.

15

Pleasingly Weird Directions

'Was that *Biro* you were talking to?' said Tori as we showered.

'Yeah,' I said breezily. I lathered my hair with loads of conditioner. 'I think he started talking to me because he sympathized about us losing our house. He lost his in Iraq.'

'A bit daft, being named after a pen,' Cazza sniggered.

'Don't be thick, Caz,' said Tori. She reached for her towel. 'It doesn't suit you.'

'He's only been in England a year,' I said. 'He actually *speaks*!'

'No,' said Tori.

'He's nice!' I protested. 'And he can't swim, just like me! He learned English at the detention centre. And he looks like a horse. Don't you think?'

'He's more like the new macaques,' Tori said. 'Specs, maybe.'

I thought about this as we all left the Kingfisher Centre in Cazza's mum's *massive* silver car. It wasn't so much that Biro looked like the macaques because he *well* looked like a horse, in a nice way, and no one was going to change my mind on that one, not even Tori. But there were other similarities. Both Biro and the macaques had been in a bad place, were now in a better place and needed to learn how to swim. It bent my brain in pleasingly weird directions.

I then realized that I'd just *thought* all this stuff and hadn't blathered it all out at Tori, who was chatting to Cazza beside me. And I'd talked to Biro entirely and totally on my own! I sat back against the soft brown car seat, feeling pleased with myself.

Tori nudged me. 'I meant to ask. Did you see me come down the Twister?'

I shook my head. 'Sorry,' I said. 'Did I miss much?'

At this rate of independence, Taya Wild, I thought, *you'll be heading down the Twister yourself next week.*

Something was crinkling in my coat pocket as we left Mum and Grandpa in the ape-house and forked left at the keepers' house called Greenings, heading for Wild World's hydrotherapy pool. It was Monday afternoon and time for the macaques' first swimming lesson. Tori was walking ahead of me, talking to Dad and Matt, with the macaques trundling along beside them in a cage on the back of Matt's electric buggy. Rabbit was keeping up as best she could. Old Bean peered through the bars at me, the white tufts of his moustache poking through the mesh. I pulled a few funny faces and he bared his teeth back in a crazy monkey smile.

Crinkle, crinkle. Crinkle, crinkle. Fishing absently in my pocket, I pulled out the swimming lessons leaflet I'd picked up at the Kingfisher Centre on Saturday. I actually stopped walking as I considered what it said.

Was it time I tried to swim again? I'd had more fun at the pool than I thought I would. OK, so that was partly down to meeting Biro and finding out that I wasn't the only person in the entire world aged eleven who couldn't swim. But the macaques were about to learn, and if a bunch of monkeys could do it, I reasoned, then surely I could as well? I pictured myself climbing the steps on the Twister and flinging myself down the slide head-first, emerging like a sparkly purple fish at the bottom to gasps of applause from my sister.

I folded the leaflet into a tiny square and put it back in my pocket. Enjoying my newly found independent-person thing, I felt no urge to rush over and tell Tori what I was thinking about. I'd sit on the idea for a while, I decided, like a chicken with a shiny leaflet-shaped egg.

The air inside the hydrotherapy pool was so gaspingly hot, I felt like we'd just been plunged into the vegetable steamer – especially when you contrasted it with the chilly December air outside.

'Excuse me while I melt like an ice-cream,' I panted at Tori. 'Could it be any hotter in here?'

'Last time I felt this hot, I was halfway up a rainforest tree trying to get a decent angle on a Malayan sun bear,' said Dad. 'We're starting in the small pool. They'll let the monkeys in any minute now.'

The hydrotherapy unit wasn't very flash, all concrete walls and steamed-up windows instead of tiled murals in tasteful blues and greens and cool music like at the Kingfisher. It was mad to think of all the animals who'd swum up and down in here, like a wild watery Animal Olympics.

We hurried over to the spectators' area: a row of

benches behind a glass dividing wall. If we looked right, we could see the big pool: the one I imagined the zebra had been swimming in. The small pool was to the left. I settled down eagerly on the bench with Tori beside me, Rabbit panting at our feet. What would the macaques think of the water? Matt said swimming would come naturally to them, but it would be weird at first. Would they freak out, or go 'WHOOPEE!' and high-five each other with their skinny monkey paws?

James, the animal physio, appeared, wearing a black rubber wetsuit and clutching a tub of fruit in his hand.

'He looks like Action Man on a picnic,' Tori said.

James *was* a bit Action Man-ish. He was Australian, with a slow smile and blond rug-like hair that looked like he combed it with a surfboard. He sat on the edge of the pool, dangling his rubber-clad legs into the water, and started chucking fruit left and right. The apple pieces floated, but several bananas sank to the bottom and shimmered at us through the water.

'I hope the macaques have brought their goggles,' I said, giggling.

'And their armbands,' said Tori, which cracked me up even more.

Old Bean appeared through a mesh flap in the wall.

He paused at the edge of the pool, holding his tail high and sniffing at the wobbly blue thing in front of him. On the opposite side of the water, James stayed perfectly still.

'Jump in, Old Bean,' I said, still snorting about the goggles and armbands thing as I willed the old macaque on.

'They've sent in the most senior monkey in the troupe.' Dad slid a camera out of his pocket and started clicking. Taking photographs was so automatic with him that he kept talking as he snapped. 'I expect they want him to set an example to the younger ones.'

The other macaques were gazing curiously at Old Bean through the mesh in the closed flap as the old monkey spotted the fruit. Chattering, he paced along the edge of the concrete, part of him keen to get the food and the rest of him cautious.

Greed won. He suddenly scampered to the steps at the far end of the pool, splashed in, grabbed the nearest bit of food and dashed out again, the fruit – a bit of apple – clutched tightly in his paw. He stopped and ate his prize, his little brown eyes darting from left to right. His moustache had got wet and was dangling down more than normal.

'Jolly good, Old Bean!' said Tori cheerfully, and I lost it all over again.

Fatso, Sparkle, Tiny and Dalek came through the flap now. They were chattering together like birds in a tree, probably saying things like, 'Are you completely mad, Old Bean?' Fatso eyed Old Bean's apple, and the old guy curled his lip in warning as if to say, 'Fetch your own, lazybones!'

'Is it just me, or does Fatso look scared of the water?' Tori said.

Fatso had a little frown on his whiskery face. He shuffled along the side of the pool and rested his paws on his bulging tummy as first Sparkle and then Dalek jumped into the water after the food. Sparkle shot straight out the other side like a well-groomed firework, chattering angrily. Dalek gazed at the pool, his snaggle tooth resting lightly on his bottom lip just like my teeth sometimes do when I'm thinking really hard, before doing this mad flump into the water and soaking Sparkle all over again. Sparkle practically went through the roof with rage.

Tori and I were wetting ourselves with laughter.

'Oh, ouch,' I gasped, leaning against the glass partition for support. 'Oh, Sparkle. That was totally fantastic.'

James threw some more fruit into the water. With a confidence twice the size of her mini self, Tiny bounced importantly down the steps and plunged straight into the pool like she'd been doing it all her life. When she came out, she was screaming with triumph – or screaming as best she could with half a banana hanging out of her mouth. Fatso shuffled away from the edge of the pool, curling his lip and looking unhappy.

'It's only a bit of water,' I called encouragingly through the glass at the tubby monkey. 'Go on. There's a little piece of apple floating just by the steps.'

Fatso had seen it. He waddled bravely towards the steps before Old Bean charged in with a scream and a growl and got the apple for himself.

Quango, Punk and Specs were the last ones through the flap. Fatso watched them glumly as one by one they clambered into the water, yelling with excitement or shock or perhaps both as they ducked down after the fruit. Punk's funky hair crest stayed sticking up even when the rest of his wet fur was plastered to his skin. He clearly used an excellent hair gel.

'Looks like we'll have to start calling you Thinso, Fats,' I informed the grumpy-looking Fatso still sitting on the edge of the pool. I hoped he'd get the hang of swimming soon. At this rate, he was going to miss his one and only shot at TV fame.

16

Feeling Really Weird Right Now

'It was *so cool*!' I enthused at Joe on Tuesday morning. 'You should have seen them, Joe. It was like they all knew right in their bones how to do it. Well, all except Fatso. How do you explain that, when all those monkeys have ever seen are the four walls of a laboratory?'

Joe's eyes were as wide as Grandpa's. He was practically on the edge of his seat. It's one of his best features, the way he listens.

'Matt's going to build a pool for them in their enclosure,' Tori added.

'And get *this*!' There was no way Tori would beat me to the punchline. 'Dad called the TV guy about the monkeys and sent him these photos that he took at their swimming lesson—'

'And the TV guy said great, he wanted to use them—'

Bam, bam, bam. Tori and I were like that game you play when you put one fist on top of the other at full speed.

'And the TV guys said their set designers would build the water feature in the macaques' enclosure—'

'For free—'

I jumped out of my seat, feeling somehow that if I was standing up Joe would hear me over Tori, and managed to kick over my chair and spill my coat and bag on the floor at the same time. 'Provided Wild World was happy to let them design it so it looked realistic and natural and they could film the monkeys swimming in it on Friday!'

'Settle down, Taya,' said Ms Hutson sharply.

I pulled my chair upright and sat, going pink in the face as I realized I'd practically been yelling towards the end of our big news. Biro grinned over his shoulder at me, so quickly that I almost missed it.

'*This* Friday?' Joe looked like he couldn't believe his ears. 'They won't build it in just four days. Will they?'

'This is *television*, Joe,' I said loftily. 'Television can do anything.'

Cazza leaned in sideways. 'Television caught me shoplifting once.'

'Exactly.' I lifted my fist to thump the table, then thought better of it because Ms Hutson was still looking at me with her 'last warning' face on.

'When were you going to tell me about this, Taya?' Tori said suddenly, holding up a shiny, crumpled bit of paper.

It was the swimming lesson leaflet. Across the top, I'd scribbled: *Tues/Thurs 4.10pm, Level 1, Learners' Pool. BE THERE!!!!* I realized it must have fallen out of my coat pocket when I sent my chair flying.

I tugged the scrawled-on leaflet from my sister's fingers, feeling flustered. 'I'd have told you last night when I fixed it with Dad and the leisure centre, only you were staying with Cazza and you weren't there.'

'You could have told me this morning,' Tor accused.

'Brain like a sieve,' I said weakly.

I'd *always* had a brain like a sieve. But Tor was usually there to catch the bits as they fell through the holes.

'Thanks for finding it,' I said, feeling as guilty as if I'd been caught stealing something. 'You know me. I'd have probably forgotten to turn up. Biro's going too.'

Tori didn't look amused by this fresh evidence that I was keeping stuff from her. *I'm not doing it on purpose!* I wanted to say. But Ms Hutson got in the way.

'"O Christmas Tree" now, Class 7H! This is our last chance to sing it through in the privacy of our classroom; we have assembly tomorrow. Don't forget red-and-white costumes on *Thursday*, please, for the dress rehearsal. And Biro? Try and join in, will you? From the top, everybody!'

Tori was unusually quiet as we stood outside the gates at the end of school. I hazarded a conversation.

'Are you going to watch the TV guys building the macaques' new water feature, then?'

Tori shrugged.

I tried again. 'Cazza not free?'

'Violin lesson.'

'You should go to Wild World, Tor,' I said. 'It'll be good! Though maybe they'll only have the digger in so it'll just be a hole and a load of earth. And I guess the macaques will be kept inside while they're doing it.'

Tori stuffed her hands deeper into her coat pockets. 'So it won't be good at all, will it?' she said.

'OK, so come and watch me in my swimming lesson!' I said. 'I'll be as bad as Fatso, you know. I'm bound to sink and need mouth-to-mouth. Or worst-case scenario, a lung transplant. And since we're the same DNA I think it's important that you're there.'

My joke bounced off Tori like a rock bouncing down a steep granite cliff. I checked my watch. I had to get a move on if I was going to make it. I could see Biro hovering at the bus stop.

'Well,' I said after a minute. 'See you back at Rob's, then.'

As I shouldered my bag and walked towards Biro, Tori called after me.

'Taya?'

I swivelled on my heel.

'Is this what you felt like when I made friends with Cazza?'

'Probably,' I said apologetically.

'See you then,' said Tor. She managed half a smile.

'Yeah, see you,' I said back.

Biro wasn't much more talkative than normal as we headed for the Kingfisher Centre together. His silence was restful. It was encouraging to know that he wasn't going to interrupt me as I went on and on about Tori.

'. . . So I think she's probably feeling really off-balance right now because that's exactly how I felt when she started hanging out with Caz. Only the difference is of course that she never wanted to make friends with *you*, no offence. But I totally get what's going on in her head and I hope she's OK, but you can't just live your life for your twin sister, can you? Did you understand any of what I just said?' I checked.

Biro waggled his hand up and down, basically meaning in the politest way: 'No, Taya, I didn't get a single word.'

We checked in at the Kingfisher Centre desk. I felt well nervous. Biro was nervous too – I could tell. He was practically *green*. He didn't look so much like a horse as a result. More like a . . .

'Why are you laughing?' Biro said as we went into the changing room.

'Because you look like a crocodile,' I snorted.

'Crocodiles can swim,' Biro pointed out gloomily.

What have I let myself in for? I thought as I chattery-teethed my way to the learners' pool five minutes later. Suddenly, swimming lessons felt like a really, really bad idea. A picture of Fatso sitting sadly on the edge of the hydrotherapy pool wafted into my mind and I slowed down, wondering how easy it would be to turn round and reach the changing room again before anyone noticed.

Biro was in the pool already. 'Your sister is here!' he

called, jabbing towards the spectators' balcony with his finger.

I stared up at the balcony. Tori was hanging over the rail, her chin on her hands. She'd come to watch me drown after all!

'Got any apples?' I shouted up at her, smiling fit to burst. 'I really need some motivation.'

Tori waggled a Mars Bar at me. Still grinning, I gave her the thumbs up and slid into the water like an otter in a sparkly purple swimming costume. Or so I like to think.

17

Well Not Pink

'Well, that was a waste of time,' I moaned as Tori and I headed up our old road to Rob's house. 'Once again, I've found something I'm totally rubbish at.'

'You sort of swam a couple of strokes at the end,' Tori said.

'My feet were touching the bottom,' I said flatly.

'Only the tips of your toenails, I expect. It doesn't count if you don't actually put your flesh down.'

'I can't believe I'm going back on Thursday for more torture,' I said unhappily.

Biro had approached the lesson with a quiet determination. He hadn't said much – no change there – but he hadn't moaned or wailed or complained or stormed off in frustration like . . . well, someone else at our swimming lesson who shall remain nameless. As a result, he'd managed more actual swimming than yours truly.

'I just don't think I'm designed for swimming,' I said tragically.

'If you mean that you don't have webbed feet, waterproof feathers or layers of insulating fat, you're right,' said Tori. 'If you did, you'd be a duck.'

'How come it was so easy for the macaques and so hard for me?'

'Probably because they didn't think about it too hard,' said Tori. 'Besides, it wasn't easy for *all* of them, was it? Fatso couldn't be lured in at all, even with zillions of bits of food bobbing around.'

'So that's the answer, then.' I knew my voice was sour. 'Stick a slice of chocolate cake on the bottom of the learners' pool and watch me swim for it.'

At Rob's, Dad was on the phone upstairs. For once he wasn't talking about swimming monkeys.

'Look, I know you're needed there, Neet, but you're needed here as well by your *family*. Remember us? . . . No . . . No, let me finish . . .'

Tori and I put our stuff down quietly by Rob's front door and took turns fussing over Doris and Rabbit, whose long yellow tails swung from side to side like a pair of furry cricket bats as they squirmed around us in bliss. The hall wasn't really big enough for us plus two golden retrievers.

'Hi, girls,' Rob beamed. He was a messy sort of man, with hair the same colour as Doris's golden-yellow coat. I couldn't really understand how happy he still was, having us all crowded into his house like sardines on a discount holiday.

'Hi, Rob.' It was hard to ignore Dad's voice as it rose higher and higher, but we did our best. 'Catch any mice today?'

'None,' Rob said. He scratched under his armpit. 'I checked the traps this morning. Funny, that.'

I couldn't decide if this was good or not. I hated to think of the little mice getting trapped, but Rob did use humane traps and released the mice at the bottom of the garden. From the constant smell, I guessed they just scuttled back inside again as soon as the coast was clear.

'Tori and Taya need you. *I* need you! . . . I know we've got the insurance money, but what am I supposed to do with it by myself? We need to *talk* about this! We have to make plans, find somewhere to live *together*. How can that not be important to you? . . . Oh, just forget it!'

Dad thundered down the stairs, stuffing his phone into his pocket, barely seeing us as he crashed out of the front door with an: 'Order pizza, girls – I can't think about food right now, for God's sake!'

Rob reversed rapidly into the living room. 'Like we even mentioned food!' Tori said indignantly as Dad whirled down the path and up the road, his shoulders set and his face screwed up like a furious old bit of newspaper. Doris and Rabbit watched him go, unsure whether to follow in anticipation of a walk.

My bad mood after the disastrous swimming lesson was getting worse. 'Dad's getting crosser and crosser and Mum's never here,' I said in despair. 'They're going to get divorced, I can feel it. Oh, why does everything always go wrong for us? You have to admit we've had more than our fair share of disasters in the past couple of months. I feel like I'm in a book that's going to have a really, really bad ending.'

The main house phone went. Rob put his head back round the living-room door. Doris bounced over to him like a large yellow beach ball.

'It's your mum,' he said, scratching Doris's ears. 'Has your dad, er, left?'

Tori took the phone from Rob while I sat down at

the bottom of the stairs with my head in my hands. Rabbit rested her heavy chin on my knee and panted at me with her hot-sock breath.

'Mum?' said Tori. 'Yeah, he's in a strop, marched out the door like he was power-walking . . . He sounded mad . . . Don't worry. Everything's going to be fine. We'll get there as soon as we can.'

'And now Mum's in tears, right?' I said through my fingers.

Putting the phone on the hall table, Tori nodded. 'She wants us up at Wild World.'

I groaned. Going out again was the last thing I felt like doing.

When was this squabbly to-and-fro life ever going to end?

You wouldn't think you could go wrong with a red-and-white dress code, would you? Big mistake.

'Your skirt is pink, Heather, not red,' said Ms Huston patiently as we lined up to file on to the stage for our dress rehearsal of 'O Christmas Tree' on Thursday morning. All nine other Year Seven classes were there as well, with their teachers rushing up and down like sheepdogs having a really bad day.

'It's *well* not pink, miss!' said Heather Cashman,

bristling and primed for a fight. 'It's *cerise*!'

'And my cousin works in fashion and she says cerise is *red* coz cherries is red and the French word for cherry is cerise!' added Carrie Taylor, making Heather nod her black curls so hard that one of her jangly gold earrings flew off and practically took Jonno Nkobe's eye out.

'Fine,' said Ms Hutson wearily. 'Tosh? A football strip doesn't constitute a Christmas concert outfit.'

'It's red and white, innit!'

'And also yellow and blue. Jonno? Did you forget . . . You forgot. Don't forget tomorrow. Catherine?'

Cazza twirled her pillarbox-red fringe casually between her fingers. 'Wassup, Miss?'

Ms Hutson already looked knackered and it was only nine thirty. She gazed unhappily at Cazza's hair. 'I hope that washes out, is all I can say.'

Getting three hundred kids on stage took half an hour. The steel band players twirled their drumsticks and checked their watches as we finally made it, balanced precariously on benches in a sea of red and white (and cerise).

'I think Ms Hutson's looking forward to the Christmas holidays,' Tori whispered to me.

'Wish I was,' I said glumly.

Dad had arranged for us to go up to Liverpool on Friday night, straight after the macaque filming. It looked unlikely that Mum would be joining us for a while. I didn't want to think about whether that 'while' would extend as far as Christmas Day itself.

'OK, we've only got ten minutes so play your part, 7H, and make it good!' Ms Hutson shouted as Mrs Longley the music teacher stepped up to conduct everyone. 'And Biro? If you're ever going to join in, now would be a good time.'

The steel band leaped into action. Together with three hundred voices, the noise was totally incredible. Having real steel drums in our school hall was like a magic cheering-up potion, and a hundred times more exciting than the CD. Music is cool like that. You get to switch your brain off from its normal daily channel because all you've got time and room for is the next line of the song.

'Good, Year Seven!' shouted Mrs Longley after we'd done it a couple of times. She sounded a bit astonished. 'Sing like that tomorrow and we'll steal the show!'

'Do you think anyone will come to see us in the concert?' Tori said as we all clattered off the stage, clearing the way for what looked like a thousand Year Eights.

'Not unless we invite Rob,' I said. 'Dad'll be in meltdown about the macaque filming in the afternoon and Mum's worked off her feet with Grandpa.'

'My mum and dad are Christmas shopping in Paris till Sunday,' said Cazza moodily. 'Like, what are they buying me? Onions?'

'My dad's working,' said Joe, in an eye-poppingly bright-red tracksuit that did nothing for his pale skin tone.

'My parents will come,' said Biro.

'Good one, Biro,' I said, forcing myself to resist the gloom that was lurking in the wings now that the music had finished and I was back on the old brain channel of worry, house, divorce. 'Four words in a public place. I think we're getting somewhere with you.'

'Why don't you sing, Biro?' said Tori curiously. 'You'd make Ms Hutson's Christmas.'

'I can't sing,' said Biro in a final-sounding voice.

'You can't swim either,' I pointed out. 'But at least you're trying.'

And then Jonno Nkobe kicked over one of the steel drums by mistake and everyone eardrums exploded.

18

Dog-Tired

'I'm thinking of giving up,' I informed Biro as we stood in the Kingfisher Centre atrium after our Thursday lesson. The back of my throat hurt where I'd snorted in half the pool and I was sure I was getting a verruca.

Biro looked shocked. 'You only did two lessons!'

'I know when I'm beaten,' I said.

'Nobody is beaten after two lessons,' Biro said.

I didn't know horses could look so fierce. 'How can you be sure?' I said lamely. Biro was already heading out into the gloomy darkness outside the leisure centre. I hurried after him. 'You're sinking nearly as much as me!'

'My grandfather told me giving up is bad,' said Biro.

'Are you close to your grandfather?' I asked.

Biro didn't say anything for ages. I thought he'd either forgotten my question or not understood me. But then:

'My grandfather is dead.'

Good one, Taya, I thought. *Now you look spineless* and *thoughtless*. 'Sorry,' I said.

'No one is beaten after two lessons,' Biro repeated as his bus swooshed up.

'OK,' I said reluctantly. 'I'll keep swimming if you try and sing in the concert tomorrow.'

Biro stuck out his bottom lip. I had an urge to feed him a sugar lump.

'Deal?' I called after him as the bus doors slid shut.

He half lifted his shoulder at me, which could have meant anything. I decided to take it as a promise. *Why is he making such a big deal about singing?* I thought crossly, watching his bus pull away. He hadn't even *tried* it. And here I was, offering to continue with something that I knew for a *fact* I couldn't do for my life!

I brooded about Biro the whole way to Wild World, and for some time after I got there too.

'You look like a wet weekend, Taya,' said Mum,

putting Grandpa over her shoulder to burp him after his milk.

'I haven't got much to look forward to, have I?' I said, full of self-pity as I dried Grandpa's milk bottle and put it back in the cupboard. 'Tori's still spending loads of time with Cazza, we haven't got a house, no one's coming to our Christmas concert tomorrow, we're not spending Christmas together and I can't swim. I'm surprised I only look like a wet weekend, Mum. I feel like a whole drizzly month.'

'What Christmas concert?' said Mum.

The thing about us all spending so little time together was the lack of communication, I'd noticed. I was *pretty* sure Tori or I would've said something to Mum and Dad about the concert – but not totally one hundred per cent guaranteed rustproof sure.

'Didn't we tell you?' I said.

Mum shook her head. She looked over my shoulder and smiled as Dr Nik came through the double doors.

'Hello, Taya,' Dr Nik said.

I liked it that he knew I was Taya, not Tori.

'Christmas concert?' Mum prompted me.

'We're not expecting you or Dad to come,' I said, 'but it's tomorrow morning. You'll be needed here for Grandpa and the filming, I expect.'

At the mention of his name, Grandpa suddenly woke up and started looking lively. Honey, the female chimp – we'd named her after the honey-coloured hairs that sprouted from her chin – came scurrying across and stood up against the glass the minute she heard the little chimp's high-pitched chattering.

'OK, Honey,' Dr Nik soothed. 'You'll get Grandpa all to yourself very soon, I promise.'

Dad came through the door of the ape-house, carrying a box of equipment with Rabbit at his side. 'Stuff from the TV people,' he panted. 'Asked if they could leave it here. They're filming the macaques from midday tomorrow. I said it would be OK. Oh, and Taya? If you and Tori want to invite some friends to watch the filming after school, that's fine. But a maximum of one friend each, OK?'

He suddenly clocked Dr Nik and stopped short, like he'd just run into a pane of glass.

'Great!' I said happily. 'I'll let Tori know. I'll probably ask Joe.'

'Did you check with Matt, Andy?' Mum said, handing Grandpa over to Dr Nik.

'Of course I checked with Matt!' Dad said, in this awful snarly voice that made me think of a tiger in a bad mood.

Mum's eyes narrowed as Dad dumped the boxes on the floor of the ape-house. One of the boxes tipped over, spilling cables on the concrete, making Rabbit yelp and scuttle off to a safe distance.

'I'm earning money for this family so we can get back on our feet after a *catastrophic* year and all I get is "Did you check with Matt?"' Dad hissed. 'This shoot with the macaques tomorrow is crucial, as I don't get the rest of my fee until everything is safely in the can. We still haven't found anywhere to live. I'm tired, I'm worried, I'm lonely. Although you don't seem to care about any of this, as your *work*' – for some reason, he glanced at Dr Nik – 'is far more important than I am!'

Mum thrust Grandpa into my arms and launched into a tirade of Portuguese at Dad. I only caught a few words, but they included things like 'selfish' and 'spoiled' and 'thoughtless', plus a few others that are best left untranslated.

Dr Nik melted away through the double doors. I tried to make myself as inconspicuous as I could, and carried Grandpa over to see Honey through the glass. Honey made her special crooning noise and tipped her head to the side as she lifted her thick black fingers in a gesture at Grandpa that said: 'I would *so* cuddle you if this invisible stuff wasn't in the way.'

Mum and Dad were really giving it some welly now, waving their arms and striding up and down. Rabbit had come over to join me and Grandpa, and was making concerned woofing noises as Grandpa pulled faces and mewled a bit.

'He's OK, Rabbit,' I said, patting the dog. 'Never mind them,' I told Grandpa bravely. 'Let's see how the TV stars are getting on.'

We moved along to the macaques' window. All eight macaques stood stock still for half a second, their heads turned towards us with interest.

'Hello, Old Bean,' I said to the old monkey, who was closest to the glass. 'Your new swimming pool looks fantastic.'

The water feature was outside, but I'd seen the set designers hard at work in the fierce glare of a heavy arc light before I'd come into the ape-house. They'd dug the pool into this deep and snakey shape, and put in an electric pump to make the water flow. Now they were adding rocks and ferns and things to make the current move in interesting directions. Incredibly, they'd planted a bunch of real full-grown *trees* beside the pool, which already looked like they'd been there for fifty years. Everything was ready for the shoot tomorrow afternoon, just like I'd told Joe it would be. He was going to love the filming. I wondered if Tori would invite Cazza, and thought she probably would.

'Another swimming lesson today, wasn't it?' I asked. 'How did Fatso get on?'

Fatso sat hunched glumly in a corner, half an apple in his paw. Old Bean chattered something at me that was probably monkey for, 'He was total rubbish.'

I shifted Grandpa to a better position and addressed the old monkey again. 'Have you learned your lines? You could be a big star, you know.'

The ape-house door slammed as Dad left. Mum took Grandpa from me with shaking hands and draped him over her shoulder. 'Your father—' she began.

'No offence, Mum,' I said, 'but I don't want to hear it. Rabbit's OK here with you for a bit, isn't she? See you later.'

I sensed Mum's concern as I headed outside, stepping over the tangle of TV cables that still lay spilled on the floor, but I was so dog-tired of everything that I didn't look back.

19

Open Mouths and Goggling Eyes

The school hall was packed for the Christmas concert. Literally. People were wedged into such tightly squeezed rows on the grey school chairs that I hoped for their sakes that no one was going to need the loo any time soon. The school hall wasn't the sturdiest-looking building in the world, with its polystyrene ceiling panels and mouldy-looking windows. I had visions of the whole place exploding if they tried to shove any extra bodies inside.

'I never knew the kids in this place had so many parents,' I whispered at Tori as we stood outside in the corridor with the rest of 7H, peering nervously through the glass window of the door that led into the hall. Behind us, the other nine classes in Year

Seven stood waiting to go on the stage as well.

'Fifteen hundred kids means three thousand parents,' said Tori. She fiddled with the Santa suit jacket she was wearing. 'Technically, anyway.'

'Two thousand nine-hundred and ninety-eight if you take away ours,' I said. 'And, well, a few less if you take away Joe's and Cazza's as well.'

'I've got four parents,' said Carrie Taylor. She sounded smug about it. 'And they're all coming. So's my cousin. How many's that, then?'

'Everyone looks terrific,' said Ms Hutson, who was wearing a pair of white furry pompoms on a red headband so she looked like a deranged poodle with its ears standing on end. 'And your skirt *almost* looks red in this light, Heather.'

'I keep telling you it's cerise, Miss!'

A deafening burst of applause exploded through the door, making us all take an involuntary step backwards.

'Dude,' said Cazza, unusually shaken out of her normal cool. 'We've not even started singing yet.'

Mr Collyer, the head teacher, had got up on the stage. He was a tall bloke who was always stooping slightly, like he was thinking about picking up something off the floor but never quite getting round to it.

'How does it start again, Miss?' said Jonno Nkobe.

There was another burst of applause. Then something else that sounded like a wave of surprise. Everyone seemed to be turning round in their seats and peering towards the back of the hall. It was hard to see properly through the window in the door and catch what everyone was staring at, but it was clear Mr Collyer was struggling to keep everyone's attention.

'What's going on out there?' said Joe.

'Maybe the back wall of the hall has just collapsed,' I suggested.

'Time to find out,' said Tori as Ms Hutson opened the door and motioned for us to lead Year Seven on to the stage.

The noise in the hall was even more deafening now that the door was open. Half the audience were standing in their seats, twisting their bodies round to look at whatever it was that had everyone going. I gazed curiously towards the back of the room as I took up my position on the stage. Someone by the doors was holding a baby. But babies weren't so interesting as to make an entire hall-full of parents practically break themselves in half in order to get a look, were they?

Then I realized.

Our mother had brought a baby chimpanzee to our Christmas concert.

'Oh my wombats!' I felt a giggle well up in my stomach like one of those big blobs you get in lava lamps. 'Tori! It's Mum! *She's brought Grandpa!*'

Mum stood at the very back of the hall, just inside the central double doors with Grandpa in her arms, his little woolly hat on his head and his hairy arms wrapped around Mum's neck as he gazed around at the sea of open mouths and goggling eyes. Heather Cashman and Carrie Taylor both shrieked, like Grandpa was some kind of savage beast about to eat them alive.

'Is that your mum?' said Cazza, peering down the hall through her bright-red fringe. 'Wicked.'

With everyone finally on stage, the steel band struck up with their great booming introduction. We all scrambled to remember what we were doing.

'*O Christmas Tree, O Christmas Tree, how lovely are your branches . . .*'

We just about had everyone's attention back by the time we reached the end of the first verse. I flashed a glance down the line at Biro. He faced forward like a stolid horse statue. His lips weren't moving an inch.

Grandpa gave one of his *whoomph*ing shouts and we

lost our audience again. Mrs Longley got us to the end of the song as best she could, though you could tell she was as desperate to look round at Grandpa as the rest of the hall was. At last, the lead drummer cheekily rounded off the end of 'O Christmas Tree' with the first bit of 'King of the Swingers' from *The Jungle Book*. There was a roar as everyone in the audience got the joke.

'I'd say we brought the house down,' Tori said as the hall shook with applause. We watched Mum and Grandpa slip back out through the double doors. 'Only I think all the credit goes to Grandpa.'

'And he didn't even sing!' Joe choked.

I couldn't believe the attention we got as we tried to get back to our classroom. All these kids I'd hardly ever seen before clustered around us in the corridors, asking questions.

'Someone said that was your mum with the chimp. Was it true?'

'Why did your mum have a baby chimp?'

'Is he your pet?'

'Couldn't you tell? It was Tori and Taya Wild's baby brother,' said Heather Cashman nastily. 'Come on, Carrie. There's a stinky monkey smell around here.'

'Chimps aren't monkeys, you brainless idiot!' Tori yelled after Cash 'n' Carrie as they flounced away.

'They're apes,' I explained to Joe, who was looking confused. I still couldn't quite believe Mum had brought Grandpa to the concert – or that she'd made it to the concert at all. 'No tails. Easy once you know how to tell the difference. Humans are apes too, by the way.'

Biro brushed past, his head down and his hands in his pockets.

'Hey, Biro!' I hurried after him. 'We had a deal, remember? I'd carry on with swimming lessons if you sang in the concert. You never even opened your lips – I saw you! You promised you would!'

Biro turned back in surprise. 'I didn't promise anything.'

'You did that shoulder shrug thing on the bus!'

Biro looked sheepish.

'Your parents came to the concert!' I said. 'I bet they loved seeing you standing there like a lemon.'

'My parents know I can't sing!'

'Well, my parents know I can't swim,' I said. 'And now I guess I'll never learn. And it's your fault.'

This was maybe a bit harsh. Between you and me, Biro was a handy excuse.

Biro opened his mouth to reply – just as Cazza stormed past us both with a murderous look on her face. I forgot my argument with Biro in a flash.

'What did you just say to Cazza, Tori?' I demanded as my sister and Joe came towards us.

Tori looked shifty. 'I invited Joe to watch the macaque filming! It's no big deal.'

'No big deal?' I echoed, processing this. 'This is Cazza we're talking about! She's not exactly known for being reasonable, is she?'

'I think she really wanted to go,' Joe said. 'She'll probably come after me now.' He tugged at the collar of his shirt, looking more than a bit scared at the prospect. Biro gave him a sympathetic look.

Folding her arms defensively, Tori said, 'Cazza Turnbull can't always get what she wants.'

'I thought I was going to invite Joe and you were going to invite Cazza!' I said.

Tori looked stubborn. 'Cazza made a dumb joke about Grandpa which annoyed me. So I asked Joe instead.'

'She looked really angry,' said Joe in anguish.

We all pictured Cazza in a rage.

'She has to learn a lesson,' said Tori at last.

'And she'll probably kick in a few toilet doors

while she's learning it,' I said.

'What is this filming?' Biro asked.

Biro was annoying and he broke promises, but now Tori'd invited Joe . . .

'Come and see for yourself, Biro,' I said with a sigh, wrenching my thoughts from Cazza and dark alleyways. 'It involves swimming. Trust me – you're going to love it.'

20

Whooping It Up Over
Banana Ice Cream

The end of term was a non-event. One minute we were all yawning at our desks and watching the clock; the next minute it was over and we were looking at a stretch of two school-free weeks. Cazza cleared off as soon as the bell went, barging past Tori and knocking her book bag off her shoulder. Tori had calmly picked up the bag and got down to discussing chess with Joe. I got a prickling sensation between my shoulderblades that I tried my best to ignore as we headed out of school together. Had all that Cazza bonding been for nothing?

'Happy Christmas to us,' sang Joe at the bus stop.

'And here comes our bus,' Tori sang back.

'Our mum fosters wild animals,' I told Biro as we climbed aboard. I felt a bit awkward all of a sudden. He knew practically nothing about our weird life apart from how we lost our house. And now he was coming to spend the afternoon with us, watching some macaques paddling up and down a pond with cameras trained on their every move. It wasn't exactly a normal playdate.

'And our dad runs an animal film business,' I ploughed on. 'Mum is fostering the little chimp you saw at school. Dad is organizing the swimming monkey film. They complement each other.'

I wondered if I'd used the right word. Mum and Dad certainly weren't complimenting each other much at the moment.

'My father is a doctor,' said Biro. 'My mother is a mother.'

'That must be nice,' I said wistfully.

I loved Mum's job – honestly I did. But it was so different now she wasn't doing it at home. Over the past few weeks, I'd got a faint sense of what Joe's life was like, with an absent mother and a dad who worked round the clock. For Joe, a nice house and a massive fridge weren't much of a pay-off – and we didn't even have *them*.

'Ooh! *Two* boyfriends today, girls!' said Charlie on the gate.

'Your flies are undone, Charlie. Did you know?' said Tori.

We left Charlie checking his trousers as we set off up the track towards the ape-house. Although it was already dark, we could see the massive arc lights from the gatehouse.

'Wow!' said Joe, blissed out as we rounded the corner. 'Hollywood!'

The macaque enclosure was alive with cameras, cranes, people in black woolly hats and high-vis jackets, clapperboards, thrumming generator engines and lots of lots of boxes piled haphazardly on the ground. Matt was looking stressed, talking on the phone and trying to deal with four TV guys all with clipboards and urgent questions at the same time. The gate connecting the enclosure to the path was wide open. The macaques had either been shut inside, or they'd escaped and were whooping it up over banana ice-cream in the café.

'Hi, Dad,' said Tori as we stepped inside the enclosure. Rabbit waddled over creakily to snuffle at us in greeting.

'Sorry I couldn't pick you up, girls,' Dad said. He looked tense, suggesting the afternoon hadn't been going well. 'It's been a little busy around here. That monkey with the belly – Fatso, do you call him? – just won't go in the water. End of term OK?'

'Hi, Mr Wild,' said Joe.

Dad nodded at Joe, then looked curiously at Biro until I hurriedly introduced him.

'Welcome to the madness of capturing animals on film, Biro,' said Dad.

Biro gazed in wonder around the empty monkey enclosure. Joe admired the water feature, which was steaming gently. Tori shoved her hands deep in her pockets and took in the scene in her usual quiet way. There was no sign of Mum. I guessed she was giving Grandpa a bottle inside the ape-house.

'Where are the macaques?' I asked.

'Inside while we sort out a boulder issue,' said Dad. He pointed at the edge of the water feature, where an artfully placed rock had slipped sideways and revealed the concrete edge of the pool. Two builders were slathering mortar on the concrete and preparing to set the boulder back in place.

'Why is smoke on the water?' Biro asked, staring at the mist rising from the pool.

'They've heated it,' Dad explained. 'These macaques are tropical animals and prefer it that way. The mist gives a nice jungly atmosphere, don't you think?' He shivered, pulling his jacket more tightly around himself. The December air was cold. 'How much more time do you think you'll need, Scott?' he called over to a guy with bristle-cut ginger hair and a row of silver earrings marching up his right ear like precious metal ants.

Scott spoke with a heavy Newcastle accent. 'Depends on whether the fat one ever gets in the water. If he doesn't, we'll have to keep him back and film without him. Shame, as he's got the kind of face viewers will like. But we can't wait much longer for him to start playing ball, Andy. Rock back in place, lads?'

The builders straightened up and brushed off their hands, nodding.

'Time to leave,' said Dad, ushering us back towards the path.

Fresh pieces of fruit were thrown into the far end of the pool. Then everyone filed out of the enclosure and gathered on the pathway outside. I realized then that all the cameras had been set up *outside* the enclosure, the lenses trained through the netting. Despite their lives in the laboratory – or perhaps because of it – the macaques were wild animals that probably didn't cope well with lots of people getting up close and personal.

The only equipment left inside the enclosure were the lights and a barely visible tunnel of fine wire mesh that connected the macaques' inside space directly with one end of the pool. With a tunnel like that in place, the macaques could only go where the TV guys wanted them to go: straight into the water.

Scott pulled out a walkie-talkie. 'Send out the monkeys,' he said into the mouthpiece.

'I'd like to have said that,' Joe said longingly. '*Send out the monkeys!* Wicked!'

Everyone fell quiet. A gate was raised inside the ape-house as Scott's signal was received, and the macaques filed out. Old Bean led the troupe as usual, with little Tiny bringing up the rear. Down the tunnel they scampered, as light as feather-footed ballerinas – apart from Fatso, who couldn't really be compared to a ballerina unless the ballerina in question was really out of shape.

'Go for it, Fatso!' I called through the mesh.

A large-ish-looking bloke on one of the cameras frowned at me.

'He thinks you meant him,' Tori whispered, giggling. Oops.

21

Monkey Hero

There was a faint mechanical noise beside me as a camera operator brought her lens closer to the action. With that much zoom, the criss-cross pattern of the netting would be completely invisible.

It looked like the swimming lessons had paid off. Old Bean splashed confidently into the pool, followed by Dalek, whose snaggle tooth was on the other side of his face and so not quite so visible as normal. Sparkle was next, sneezing prettily as a bit of water went up her nose. Quango and Specs squabbled a bit on the edge, but they splashed in after a few seconds.

When it came to Fatso's turn, he chattered and sidled around like a horse that doesn't want to jump over a fence. I could feel the tension of everyone watching.

'Come on,' I muttered again, biting the side of my thumb. 'It's only water, Fatso. I wish I had your natural swimming ability – you don't know how lucky you are. Give it a try!'

Punk squealed crossly behind Fatso, making him jump with surprise. He slid clumsily into the water. Everyone out on the path breathed in sharply.

'Yay!' Tori mouthed at me as Fatso put one paw in front of the other and started swimming, hesitantly at first and then more strongly, after his troupe.

Fatso had done it! Scott the director raised his eyes to the sky in thanks and Dad did a little jig beside me on the path. What a monkey hero!

I vowed right then and there to try harder at my swimming. Only wimps gave up after two lessons. Fame and fortune might not have been waiting for me on the other side of the Kingfisher Centre pool like it was for Fatso on the other side of the Wild World water feature, but for Fatso's sake – and for Biro's too – I was going to stop complaining.

Filled with this new sense of purpose, I grinned broadly at Biro. He was too busy staring at the wires and buttons on a nearby camera to grin back.

Punk and finally Tiny made the line of monkeys complete. They swam across the pool, their tails slightly raised out of the water and their little heads bobbing along like a watery row of nodding dogs. Sparkled sneezed again. There was enough fruit for all of them at the far end, although I noticed Old Bean made a few warning grimaces at Tiny when the small monkey tried to snatch a bit of apple out from under his nose. Fatso looked like he was in shock, and only ate a tiny bit of pineapple.

Scott the director brought his hand down and the cameras clicked off.

'Good work, everyone!' Scott sounded pleased. 'I'll just run through what we've taken and decide if we need more footage. Take five!'

A sigh rippled around the edge of the enclosure as twenty-five people all let out the breath they'd been holding.

'Brilliant!' said Joe, grinning from ear to ear.

'Very interesting,' said Biro, admiring the cogs and joints underneath the nearby camera that made the equipment rise and fall at the touch of a button.

Five minutes later, Scott gave the all-clear – the signal that he'd taken all the footage he needed. Joe's face was a picture of disappointment as the macaques swam back across their pool – even Fatso – and up the fine mesh tunnel to their monkey house, obviously keen to get out of the cold evening air.

'That was quick,' he said sadly.

'You haven't been here since midday, Joe,' said Dad, sounding jubilant. 'Great job, everyone! Thanks, Scott!'

The director raised his hand in acknowledgement. The crew began dismantling their equipment and winding up a million miles of cabling. And as soon as the signal came from the ape-house that the macaques were safely shut inside, the enclosure gate was opened and heavies started taking the great arc lights down.

'There's Mum!' said Tori suddenly.

Mum and Dr Nik came towards the enclosure together. Grandpa was wrapped up in a kind of sling on Mum's front, his hat pulled firmly down around his great big ears. As they got closer, we could see that Grandpa was asleep and sucking his thumb. Rabbit trotted up to Mum, reaching up to sniff Grandpa in her usual motherly way.

'How did the filming go?' Mum said as we crowded around and cooed over the little chimp. Biro was fascinated. It was the first time he'd seen Grandpa up close.

'Fine,' said Dad shortly. 'As you'd have discovered if

you'd come earlier. Been busy in the ape-house, have you?'

'Dad!' Tori began.

'Dad!' I said at the same time, dissolving with embarrassment. Did they have to do this now, in front of Joe and Biro?

Dad stalked away from Mum and Dr Nik into the enclosure. Looking furious, Mum clutched Grandpa to her chest and marched after him.

'Parents are so embarrassing,' Tori said tightly, stroking Rabbit.

'Yes,' I said with feeling. 'Sometimes I wish they were nothing to do with us.'

'It's OK,' said Biro. Joe's ears had turned red, though that was possibly because of the cold air.

We watched Mum and Dad hissing at each other like two angry geese beside the macaques' pool. It was just *awful*. What made it worse was that everyone else had started noticing that something was wrong. Matt, Dr Nik, Scott the director . . .

'Let's go and get something to eat at the café,' said Tori.

'Best idea you've had all day,' I muttered.

Then catastrophe struck.

Jabbing the air with her finger, Mum practically ran

at Dad like she was about to clonk him on the jaw and knock him to the ground. Her foot connected with the dodgy rock beside the macaques' pool, which rolled off the still-wet mortar; she did this sort of lurch – and poor little Grandpa catapulted out of his sling and plunged into the water.

Everyone stood, paralysed by what had happened. Everyone apart from me.

'GRANDPA!' I tore into the enclosure, pulling off my jacket, wrenching off my shoes. 'GRANDPA!' Then I hurled myself into the pool after the tiny chimp. Had he drowned? Was I too late?

As the water closed over my head and went up my nose, dimly I heard Tori scream: 'What are you doing, Taya? *You can't swim!*'

22

Dying Fish

Almost as soon as I was completely submerged, I realized what a crazy thing I'd just done. I flailed about, coughing and panicking. The pool was deep – I knew that, because I'd seen them digging it. Every few seconds I managed to snatch some air before I sank again. Ninety-nine per cent of my brain was totally flipping out. But somehow the one per cent that was still calm and collected kept tapping out its little message. *Save Grandpa. Save Grandpa. Save—*

My fingers connected with some fur under the water. I grabbed a handful of wet, hairy skin. Now swimming was even harder because I only had one arm to do it with. But there was no way I was letting go.

Someone grabbed my sleeve and yanked me

upwards. 'Kick, Taya!' I heard Mum say, her voice high and terrified. 'Pull him up!' Water was everywhere: in my eyes, up my nose, in my mouth. My clothes felt heavy; my limbs totally uncoordinated. 'You've got him! Good girl!'

With a massive effort, I heaved Grandpa up through the water one more time. He popped above the surface, coughing and hiccuping in confusion, his sopping fur plastered this way and that over his wet little head. Someone pulled him out of my grip. With all the grace and dignity of a dying fish, I flopped my way to the edge of the pool. I didn't have a single drop of energy left.

A forest of arms pulled me out. I collapsed on the side of the pool, coughing my guts out. Wombats, it was cold. Suddenly I wanted to be back in the heated water again.

'Someone get a towel!' Dad shouted.

A wave of towels and blankets were wrapped around me. 'Grandpa!' I croaked, struggling through the folds. 'Where's Grandpa? I want to see Grandpa!'

'The kid wants her grandparents,' said someone from the film crew. 'Are they here?' It would have been funny if the situation hadn't been so awful.

'He's fine,' said Tori, crouching beside me. 'Dr Nik's

taken him into the nice warm ape-house to check him over. Rabbit's gone too, like *she* can help.'

'That was the bravest thing I've ever seen!' Joe's eyes were bugging out of his head. 'We thought you were going to drown!'

I coughed weakly. 'That water tastes disgusting.'

'You probably swallowed some monkey poo,' said Tori.

That made me feel even weaker. 'Oh, *gross!*' I wailed.

A horrible noise started up somewhere near the bank of cameras. Vaguely I wondered if Wild World had moved their hyenas next door to the macaques.

'*O Christmas Tree,*' sang Biro by the gate. '*O Christmas Tree. How lovely are your branches.*'

And I knew he was doing it for me to say sorry for being such a wimp in the concert, especially since I'd just done possibly the stupidest – or bravest, depending on how you want to look at it – thing in the entire history of Taya Wild. And believe me, this was up against some pretty stiff competition.

'Blimey,' said Tori. 'Biro's right. He can't sing at all.'

When we'd all extricated ourselves from the final clear-up and the macaques had been fed and put to bed and

Dad had signed various bits of paper and Dr Nik had declared Grandpa fit and well and the trucks had rumbled off down the service road taking Scott and all his crew back to their glamorous TV lives, Matt invited us all back to his house to recover.

The house was large and white, with a wavy black roof that sank almost to the ground on either side like a pair of extremely beetly black eyebrows, and was tucked round behind the zebras in the quietest corner of the park – the bit which backed on to Fernleigh Common.

'Didn't we have a dolls' house like this once, Tori?' I said, gazing admiringly at the floodlit white face of the house as we all trooped up the gravel path.

Matt unlocked the front door and waved us inside. 'There are several like it dotted around the park. It came with the job.'

Dr Nik followed me, Tori, Joe and Biro inside, carrying Grandpa. The chimp's fur was fluffy and clean, his eyes bright. He clung on to Dr Nik's front and chattered softly. He didn't look any the worse for his watery little adventure.

Since his horrible outburst of singing, Biro had got strangely talkative. 'Is it nice living in the wildlife park?' he asked Matt now. 'Do you hear the animals in the night? Do you think you are living in Africa sometimes?'

'I do have some funny dreams, I'll tell you that,' Matt admitted.

Last ones through the door were Rabbit, Mum and Dad. I'd never seen our parents so quiet in my life. They looked like they'd shrunk. Dr Nik made to hand Grandpa over to Mum. Mum took a step backwards and shook her head.

'I can't take him, Jonas,' she said.

Grandpa gurgled and reached for Mum, just like a rather furry baby that's pleased to see someone. Rabbit woofed hopefully.

'Of course you can, Anita,' said Dr Nik. 'He needs you.'

'Everyone makes mistakes,' Matt put in as Dad watched with dark eyes. 'Anyway, you could argue that the TV crew didn't mortar in that rock properly. And the sling is clearly faulty to have come apart so easily.'

'I shouldn't have taken Grandpa into the enclosure in the first place.' Mum passed her hand over her eyes. 'When I think about how unprofessional I was, I want to die of shame. Grandpa might have . . . might have . . .'

Dad reached over to put his arm round Mum's

shoulders. Mum shook him off.

'This is really my fault,' Dad said, not sure what do with his arm now. He flexed his fingers and put his hand in his pocket. 'I shouldn't have started an argument in front of everyone the way I did.'

'And I'm sorry for putting you all under such pressure in the first place,' Matt said. 'I didn't appreciate how difficult things would be, so soon after your house fire. I should never have asked Anita to foster the little chimp. It's just – she's the best foster carer I know.'

This was like Apology Central. I wondered who'd say sorry next. Dr Nik? Grandpa?

Mum still hadn't taken Grandpa from Dr Nik's arms. 'It is time for me to give up, Matt,' she said. 'I need to be with my girls. We must start rebuilding our house or selling the land or something – and find somewhere to rent so we can live together properly again. I can't foster animals in someone else's property. And today has taught me that I cannot be trusted with the little ones any more.'

'Don't give up, Mum!' I said in alarm. A Wild family without wild animals in their lives would be all wrong!

'The animals need you,' Tori said. 'Look at Grandpa!' The little chimp had started whimpering. He was still stretching out his little arms towards Mum, bewildered that she wasn't giving him a cuddle.

'I'm sorry.' Tears gleamed in Mum's eyes. 'It's for the best.'

'You need to be with your *girls*?' Dad said suddenly. 'What about *me*?'

23

Lost Hikers on a Mountainside

'Is someone going to get a tumour next?' I demanded as I strode up and down Matt's gravelly path in the chill and the dark. The floodlights sent my shadow scooting up the house's white walls like a leggy *Scooby Doo* ghost. Joe, Biro and Tori all watched me silently from their various positions on Matt's front lawn. We'd decided to wait outside for things to calm down, as Mum and Dad had started shouting at each other again. 'Maybe there'll be an earthquake. I mean, what else can go wrong?'

Joe, Biro, Tori and I all jumped out of our skins as Matt's front door slammed so hard it almost came off its hinges.

'You are a silly, jealous man!' Mum shouted,

wrenching the door open again as Dad came towards us down the path, pulling his head into his shoulders the way a tortoise goes into its shell. 'Go to Liverpool, spend Christmas away from here! And DON'T COME BACK!'

'That?' said Tori as Dad flung open the gate and disappeared into the gloom without even looking back at us.

'Oh wombats,' I said in dismay. 'It happened. I *knew* it would happen! *Mum just dumped Dad!*'

Joe's eyes looked dark and solemn in the weird orange light, the heavy shadow of his nose falling sideways across his cheek like a badly fitting superhero mask. He clutched his book bag tightly to his chest.

'They are just angry,' said Biro. 'My parents fight all the time but they are fine.'

'There's fighting, and there's Fighting,' I said. I was feeling tearful now. 'And believe me, *that* was Fighting.'

'Do you think Dad's really going to Liverpool without us?' said Tori.

We listened for any sign that Dad was coming back to make up with Mum. Nothing.

'Looks that way,' I said, swallowing.

'So that's it then,' said Tori in a strange voice. 'No

house, no parents, no animals.'

'No Christmas,' I added bitterly. 'And Cazza waiting to beat us up around every corner in Fernleigh from now until for ever.'

The awfulness of our future soaked into our souls the way I once saw a large blob of acid soak into a wooden worktop in the school lab.

'You should go back in,' said Joe at last.

I wanted to rewind everything to around about the point where Mum and Dad started fighting in the macaques' enclosure. But I couldn't, so I did what Joe said.

My fingers were trembling so hard I almost couldn't turn the front door knob. When I finally pushed the door open and fell into the hall, I saw Mum weeping into Dr Nik's shoulder. Matt was standing beside them, joggling Grandpa in his arms, while Rabbit lay with her head on her paws looking resigned.

'Taya!' Mum sobbed, seeing me. 'Your father has gone!'

She fell against me and burst into a fresh round of crying. Grandpa's little face puckered up and he started making sad little noises in Matt's arms. Matt soothed and joggled him some more while talking to Dr Nik in a low voice. I couldn't catch what they were saying over Mum's tears.

I fought the lump of tears back down my throat. *Be more like Tori*, I instructed myself. *Don't cry.* 'You told him to, Mum,' I said, looking apologetically over her head at Joe and Biro. 'Phone him. Ask him to come back. You can sort this out if you just talk to each other!'

'Your father is wrong,' Mum snarled, her feisty side popping out of the sobbing mess for a moment. 'He must come to *me*.' She peered over my shoulder with red eyes. 'Where is Tori?'

Why did everyone always ask that question? I wondered if they ever asked Tori the same thing about me. I'd never know the answer to that one, I supposed, because if I was there to hear the question, it would be a pointless question.

Pulling my brain back as it rambled about like a bunch of lost hikers on a mountainside, I looked around the room for Tori. She wasn't there.

'I don't think she came inside,' Biro offered.

I detached myself from Mum and went out into the darkness again with Rabbit lumbering enthusiastically beside me. 'Tori?' I called across the silent orange-lit garden. I had an unsettling feeling that something was seriously wrong. I mean, more seriously wrong than our lives exploding almost as loudly as our house. 'Tor? Are you there?'

Was this the sixth-sense twin thing kicking in? I'd always wanted that to happen because it sounded cool in books and films. But the swirling in my stomach like I'd eaten too many McFlurries wasn't cool at all.

Mum and Matt, Dr Nik and Grandpa, Joe and Biro followed me and Rabbit as we zigzagged across the lawn, like a straggle of puppies following a couple of bloodhounds. Rabbit woofed joyfully. A walk in the dark was her idea of heaven.

'Tori? Tor?'

'What was the last thing you remember Tori saying?' Mum asked, her voice rising.

'She made this list about the stuff that was wrong,' I said, wishing the sick feeling would go away. 'It was six words long, but it said everything.' Apart from a couple of extra nightmares I'd thrown in there for good measure, I added silently to myself. 'Typical Tori,' I said out loud.

I stopped short at the end of the garden. The gate leading to Fernleigh Common was banging weakly against its hinges.

'She's gone on the common,' I said, realizing this

almost as if a large photo of Tori had appeared on the horizon with a big neon arrow saying *THIS WAY!* very loudly, possibly with accompanying music and dance routines.

'What?' said Joe.

'But it's dark there,' said Biro. 'She can't see anything.'

Mum gasped. I knew at once that she had thoughts of the steep quarry pit and the boggy bits, murderers and kidnappers, crocodile-infested swamps, swirling river currents and ravening hyenas freshly escaped from Wild World all romping round her head, because I had those exact same thoughts too.

I pulled open the gate and started to run into the darkness. 'We have to find her *now*!' I screamed. 'Are you coming or am I doing this all by myself?'

I came back after about twenty seconds.

'Anyone got a torch?'

Dr Nik took Grandpa back to the ape-house while Matt located a heavy chrome torch, which he flashed about like he was signalling to aliens.

'I am calling the police!' said Mum, pale and shaking as she tried to stab 999 into her phone in the darkness.

'I hope that you are right, Taya,' said Biro as we struggled over the tussocks and lumps of the common

170

in the beam of Matt's torch.

'Me too,' said Joe, following. 'The police don't like to be called if the person isn't missing at all but just having a drink in the café. Do you think we should call the café in case?'

'I'm right,' I said passionately. 'It's hard to explain, I think maybe it's the twin thing, but I know I'm right so you've got to believe me.' I paused. 'Anyway, the café'll be closed by now. But maybe we should get Mum to call the security guards at Wild World. You know, just in case. TORI! TORI!'

'TORI!' Everyone took up the cry.

The common looked totally different by torchlight – especially this bit, which we didn't know as well as the part behind our house. Trees took on creepy shapes and every few steps I expected to fall down into the invisible quarry pit. The ground buckled and squirmed beneath our feet, catching us out as we stumbled on bits of rough ground that looked perfectly flat but were actually hiding great deep squelchy dents.

'TORI!'

It was hard to believe this was the same normal, occasionally dull, frequently littered place where we'd walked Rabbit and assorted wild animals for years and years. Matt swept his torch backwards and forwards, startling rabbits and beer cans and bushes with the bright, rushing light.

'There's our old road,' I said, pointing at the glimmering horizon after about ten minutes. 'Keep heading that way. I think she may have gone back to the house.'

'Where are the tiger cubs when you need them?' Joe joked nervously, his eyes darting into every strange shadow that we passed.

'Did you say "tiger cubs"?' said Biro.

Explaining took another ten minutes.

'TORI! TORI!'

The row of lights signalling our road was getting closer. Behind us I could hear Mum arguing into the phone. 'She went missing maybe twenty minutes ago. Yes, that is what I said! But she is *missing*! She is eleven years old and she is *missing*! I cannot call again in twenty-four hours! She may be *dead* in twenty-four hours!'

I was the first to see Tori's silhouette against the back gate of what was left of our old house. The weak moonlight was falling in a particular way on the ground, or I wouldn't have seen her at all. Clearly she wasn't about to shout about being there, even thought she must have heard us yelling for at least the past five minutes.

Waving at the others to tell them to stay quiet, I jogged over to her. We stood side by side for a bit, contemplating the black ruins.

'Not much of a view,' I said.

'I'm thinking, not looking,' Tori answered.

'What about?'

'About how everything can go before you even notice. I loved our life before, Taya – you know? I totally loved this house and all our animals and everything. And everything went bang, just like that. And now Mum and Dad have gone bang as well.'

She broke into great heaving sobs. I mean, really massive ones like a stormy sea was washing through her. Then she sort of curled over like a snail with her hands wrapped around her tummy and she roared some more. And when she finished, she stood up straight and wiped her eyes and said, 'I needed that.'

'What do I always tell you?' I said smugly.

Mum came rushing up – 'Tori!' – and wrapped Tor up in the kind of hug she really hates. Matt took the phone from Mum's hand and apologized to the police and turned it off before slipping it back into Mum's pocket. Joe and Biro just looked relieved.

We heard the sound of Doris barking her paws off over Rob's back gate. Rabbit howled back with gusto. The walk on the dark common had brought out the wolf in her.

'Perhaps your old neighbour can make us all a cup of tea,' suggested Matt.

I linked arms with Tori and we followed Mum, Matt and Rabbit up Rob's garden path. Biro and Joe walked beside us.

'Sorry everything's been a bit weird,' I said to Biro. 'Some filming, some shouting, me nearly drowning, my parents breaking up and Tori getting lost. We'll do something more normal next time.'

Doris was barking like one of those electronic dog-bark doorbells you can get which go on and on and on if you hold your finger on them. When Mum rapped on the back door, Rob opened up with a look of shock on his face.

'Am I glad to see you, Anita,' he said. 'I've just found two snakes in my airing cupboard.'

24

Sun After Rain

'It's a sign that everything's going to be OK!' I said jubilantly, as we stared enraptured at the two taped-up cardboard boxes with little breathing holes stabbed through the top with a pencil which contained our snakes. 'Fernando and Sufi *survived*, Tori! I mean, can you believe it?'

Joe and Biro had left for their nice normal snake-free homes after lots of polite 'Thank you for having me – I've had a very interesting time's, particularly from Biro. Tori and I had barely waved them off before we rushed back up to our room, where Mum had told us we could keep the snakes for the night – on strict instructions from a porridge-faced Rob about making sure the boxes were taped up really tightly.

'Mum totally snapped out of her Dad funk, didn't she?' I said. 'I thought she was going to give Fernando a full-on kiss.'

Tori rocked back on Rob's lumpy sofabed. 'It explains why Rob stopped catching mice in his traps,' she said.

'And why his house doesn't smell so mousey any more,' I added. 'He's probably really grateful to Fernando and Sufi for eating them all. Maybe he's even thinking of getting a pet snake to keep his mouse population under control in the future!'

'I don't think Doris would like that very much,' said Tori.

Doris had gone totally ballistic when we finally extracted Fernando and Sufi from the lovely cosy nests they'd made for themselves in the squishy orange foam lagging wrapped round Rob's hot-water tank. She'd barked so much that she lost her voice. When we came up to bed, Mum carrying Sufi and Tori and I carrying Fernando between us, we'd left Doris lying pathetic and exhausted beside Rabbit on the kitchen floor at Rob's feet.

I stared ecstatically at the two boxes on the worn carpet. 'I can't believe they're really in there,' I said.

'Well, don't go checking.' Tori turned over, trying to

get comfortable. 'They might escape in the night and freak poor Rob and Doris out all over again.'

I smiled into the darkness. 'Night, Tori.'

There was a moment when I knew we were both thinking of Dad, driving his lonely way up the motorway to Liverpool.

'Night, Taya,' Tori said back.

On Saturday morning, the sun came out. Properly out. The world was completely drowned in colour as the yellow light made the dead leaves fizz on the Fernleigh Common trees outside the spare-room window and the grasses look like yellow clotted cream. It made me realize that we hadn't seen proper colours for weeks and weeks because of the grey clouds making everything look like those so-called magic painting books, which are grey until you put water on them and make them colourful. My eyes were practically doing flips as I came bounding down the stairs with Tori to forage for breakfast in Rob's fridge.

'It's another sign,' I said happily. 'Light after dark, sun after rain, you know. Everything's going to work out.'

'How?' Tori said.

'I don't know the details, do I?' I said. 'I've just got a

Good Feeling. With capitals.'

In the kitchen Mum was standing at the sink, staring out at his back garden. The snake boxes were both on the wide window sill in front of her. Her hair was a bit lank, like she hadn't washed all the conditioner out properly, and her shoulders were hunched. She was back in a Dad funk again.

The phone rang, making Rabbit and Doris both bark their heads off. *Dad!*

'I've got it!' I shouted over the racket, even though Mum didn't turn round.

'Tori? Taya? It's Matt. Is your mum there?'

'It's Taya,' I said, swallowing my disappointment that it wasn't Dad on the other end. 'And Mum's here in body but not in spirit, if you know what I mean.' I laid the phone down on the table and said Mum's name three times before she looked round.

'Matt's on the phone,' I said, hating to crush the look of hope on her face.

Mum went out the back door with the phone pressed to her ear.

'Do you think Matt's trying to get Mum to change her mind again about fostering Grandpa?' Tori asked, biting into a piece of toast.

'Hope so.' I watched Mum carefully through the

kitchen window, trying to read her face. But she had her back to me as she paced around. 'Although Dr Nik was saying last night that it's nearly time to hand Grandpa over to Honey and the other chimps so they probably don't need her for much longer.'

Mum had stopped in the middle of the lawn, one foot raised in the air like it couldn't decide whether to go forwards or backwards. Her arm dropped to her side and dangled there, the phone loosely hanging from her fingers like a fat seed pod about to drop off its tree.

'Now what?' Tori came over beside me to watch as Mum walked very slowly back towards the house.

'Dunno,' I said, perplexed.

'Get your coats, girls.' Mum had this strange expression on her face as if her eyes and her mouth hadn't quite got together and worked out what look they were trying to achieve. She put Rob's phone down on the kitchen table. 'Rabbit? Time for a walk.'

Rabbit creaked around in delight as Mum pulled the lead from her pocket and attached it to Rabbit's collar with shaking fingers.

'Mum, what's up?' I was starting to feel alarmed. 'What's going on?'

'Tori, tell Rob we're walking to Wild World,' said

Mum. 'The sun is out. We need some air. Yes?'

'Yes, but—' I began.

'Yes, Mum but—' said Tori.

Mum was already outside again, pulling on her coat as she walked. Tori and I looked at each other, shrugged, then dashed to the hall to grab our coats.

'See you later, Rob!' Tori shouted up the stairs.

'We're off to see the wizard!' I felt like adding.

There was definitely something Oz-like going on here. The sun beamed down on us like it was in on some special secret as we took the path across the common that we'd covered the night before. I swear the grasses were whispering and watching us pass.

I couldn't shake the feeling that we were heading for something momentous.

Mum was striding ahead at the sort of speed that was starting to bother Rabbit, who kept getting yanked off her feet as Mum soldiered on without looking back to check whether Rabbit was sniffing stuff or having an old-dog sit-down.

'Do you think it's worth asking exactly what Matt said on the phone?' Tori asked me, tramping through the sparkling dew that glittered on the ground in front of us.

'Nope.' I turned my face up to the sun, enjoying the

warmth on my cheeks. 'Tori?' I said as the thought struck me. 'What exactly did you say to Cazza that first day? You know, when a word from her made "O Christmas Tree" cool enough for everyone to sing?'

'I said I'd show her my signed Christopher Ecclestone postcard if she spoke up,' Tori said. 'He wasn't the Doctor long enough to sign loads of postcards so it's quite rare. I figured out she was *Who*-mad when I saw the Cybermen stickers on her bag.'

'But your postcard was burned,' I said.

Tori shrugged. 'She didn't know that, did she?'

'When did she find out?'

'About half an hour later.'

'And she didn't mind that you'd tricked her?' I said, astounded.

'Of course she minded,' said Tori. 'But she got over it. She phoned last night, by the way. I think you were watching *The Wizard of Oz*. We're mates again, which is a relief because I didn't really want to get beaten up next term. Besides, she promised me ages ago that she'd lend me all her *Who* DVDs.'

We walked on a bit more.

'This is so weird,' I confessed. 'Finding out stuff you've known about but I haven't right up till this moment.'

'I felt like that when you fixed up those swimming lessons with Biro.' Tori shot me a sideways glance. 'So we're OK about having different friends now?'

I thought about my old helium balloon for a split second. But Tori wasn't going anywhere. She was just stretching out sideways.

'I guess,' I said.

We skirted the old quarry pit and the boggy bits of the path and reached Matt's back gate, panting at the mad pace Mum had set us all. Rabbit looked about ready to keel over.

'Are we having a cup of tea with Matt, Mum?' I said, hurrying to catch the gate before it swung closed on us.

'Matt's really into tea,' Tori added. 'Have you noticed?'

Mum motored on through Matt's garden. I imagined I could see small propellers on her wellies, pushing us all along to wombat knows where. Tori and I started guessing at random.

'Chimpanzee enclosure?' Tori panted as we approached the wired-in trees. Honey and the others gazed out at us as Mum strode on.

'Nope,' I panted back. 'Macaques?'

Tori turned her head, watching the macaques

playing in their swimming pool. Fatso was preparing to do a show-off dive from the side. 'Nope.'

Mum looked like she was heading for the tigers.

'Don't tell me Chips and Gravy have come back again,' I said, clutching at my side. It was starting to hurt.

Just before the tigers, Mum swung a sharp left towards Greenings and the hydrotherapy pool. Smoke was twirling out of Greenings' chimneys. I realized I'd never seen smoke there before.

'We're taking Rabbit for a swim?' Tori hazarded.

Matt was waiting at the gate of Greenings, flanked by two tall laurel hedges. A set of keys were swinging on his fingers.

'That was quick!' he said, looking a little surprised as Mum wrapped him in a silent bear hug and smothered his round red cheeks with kisses. 'I've lit the fire, though the boiler will take a little time to get going. Come in and take a look at your new home. I've put the kettle on.'

25

Ballerina in a Music Box

I didn't know where to put myself. I was like that awkward-shaped book you've probably got that doesn't fit with the other books on your bookshelf because it's too tall or too long or . . .

'Pinch me,' I moaned, when my head returned from orbiting the world at the speed of light. 'Pinch me, Tor.'

'Seriously?' said Tori.

I nodded. 'Seriously. OW! Oh my wombats, this is *really real*!'

While I rubbed my arm, Tori went back to sucking in Greenings with her eyes like a greedy Hoover. Matt stood with Mum talking about radiators and phone lines and plumbing. I walked into the big wooden kitchen, feeling like I had too many arms and legs and heads.

'How?' I reached out and touched the wooden kitchen surfaces, all clean and shiny and smelling of polish. 'Why?'

'. . . the timer switch is in the cupboard under the stairs . . .'

'This is really going to be ours?'

'. . . dodgy cesspit but it goes with the territory, these houses...'

'MATT!' I shouted. 'MUM!'

Mum and Matt stopped talking and looked at me. My heart was about to burst out of my ribcage, it was thumping so hard.

'*How have we got this house?*'

'We used to rent it to one of our keepers – a girl called Sarah,' Matt explained. 'She went on a sabbatical to Kenya six months ago, working on a rhino project out there. We were expecting her back in the New Year, but she called yesterday and told me she'd been offered a job out there and wouldn't be coming back.' He spread his arms, making his black-and-white Wild World polo shirt stretch alarmingly across his belly. 'After what Anita said about being unable to foster animals in someone else's property, it sank in that this house was now free and perfect for the job. I should have thought of it straightaway. But there was rather a lot going on, as I recall.'

'Don't you have to give it to someone who works here?' Tori asked, still standing like a statue in the hallway.

Matt beamed. 'Your mother has just accepted the job that goes with the house,' he said. 'We've jiggled it around a bit so that she'll automatically get a smaller workload whenever we have a youngster in need of her special attention.' He looked at Mum. 'Like right now.'

'I have agreed to foster Grandpa again until he is ready for life with Honey and the other chimps,' Mum explained. Her smiling teeth shone like pearls in the light pouring through the leaded panes on the kitchen window. 'I couldn't take the house without the babies, could I?'

'I guess not,' I whispered. I was doing my best to take everything in without spinning on the spot, round and round like a ballerina in a music box.

'When your mother isn't fostering, we'll be keeping her busy on the site with other things,' said Matt. 'So what do you think, girls?'

I sank to my knees, then down on to my face, laying

my cheek on the kitchen's polished brick floor. It felt cold on my skin, soothing me like chilled water on a burn. 'We're staying,' I mumbled at the floor. 'We can see the animals before school every day.' I jerked my head up. 'Can we get discounts at the shop and the café?'

'Of course,' said Mum.

I think I actually groaned at this.

'Get up, you weirdo.' Tori hauled me to my feet. 'I want to choose our room.'

We charged back into the hall and up the shallow wooden stairs with their curly wooden banisters.

'This one!' I shouted, skidding into a room with a sloping ceiling and a view of the emus grazing peacefully in their field.

'No, this one!' Tori called back, already halfway up to the room in the attic. 'You can see the tigers!'

I rushed after her. The attic room was massive, with wooden beams and two long windows that swept down to the floor. Sure enough, we could see Sinbad twitching his tail as he gazed over his little kingdom. It knocked spots off our old view of other people's curtains and maybe a blackbird on the TV aerial opposite.

'You don't have to share if you don't want to!' Mum

called up the stairs. 'There are three bedrooms.'

I lay down on the attic-room floor with my chin in my hands and gazed out at Wild World over the top of the long laurel hedge. Tori lay down next to me.

'We're fine sharing, Mum!' I shouted back.

'As long as I can have the bed nearest the window,' Tori said.

'There's two windows,' I pointed out, surprised my sister hadn't noticed. 'We can have one each.'

'Duh,' said Tori with a giggle.

Wild World, Wild World, Wild World. We live at Wild World, Wild World, Wild World. We live at . . .

It took me days to get this out of my head. I was chanting it as we packed our (very few) belongings and said goodbye to a surprisingly sad Rob and Doris. I was humming it as we installed Fernando and Sufi in Wild World's tropical house: Mum had given them to the zoo as a thank-you. I was singing it as the removals lorry came and took away Sarah the ex-keeper's furniture on Monday morning, leaving us with this amazing empty house that was now totally *ours*. I mumbled it on every step up and down the attic stairs and the main stairs, and thought it with every stride around the park as we met our new neighbours and got our heads round our new lives. Even the sound of the new key in the wooden front door set me off. Each day was literally a trip to the zoo.

Our first night, we only had mattresses for beds. But that night in our attic room was possibly the best night *ever*. I only wish I'd been awake to enjoy the fact that I was asleep, if you know what I mean. We were in our new house – Greenings, Wild World, Fernleigh. The only thing missing was Dad. And furniture.

On Wednesday morning, Mum told us we were going shopping.

She settled Grandpa into the crook of her neck where he burped quietly and clutched a long strand of Mum's dark hair in his hairy little fist. A bottle of finished milk lay on the side. 'We need six chairs, *queridas*,' Mum said, gesturing at the empty kitchen with her free hand. 'A table too. A sofa, armchairs. Beds. Wardrobes. The insurance from the fire will pay for everything. It is Christmas Day on Friday and I want everything to look like a real home.'

I started giggling helplessly. I get a bit like that when shopping is mentioned, especially on this kind of scale.

'It's a shame Dad can't come shopping with us,' said Tori.

Mum busied herself with adjusting Grandpa's nappy.

'That is the way of things just now, Tori,' she said without looking up.

'Has Dad called at all?' I asked hopefully.

'Come,' Mum said in this extra-bright voice, avoiding my question, 'we will hand Grandpa over to Dr Nik for the afternoon and then take the bus to town. We are rich ladies today, OK? We can spend, spend, spend.'

26

A Bit of Christmas Telly

And then suddenly the pale light of Christmas morning was filtering through our new bright-green bedroom curtains.

'What do you think Dad's doing today?' asked Tori, as she unwrapped a *Doctor Who* annual from her stocking.

I propped myself up in the new bed, stroking my new teddy chimpanzee. 'Missing us, with any luck,' I said. 'He's a right idiot, not being here for all of this.' I gestured at our bedroom with its lovely curtains, our matching beds and the round white-and-green rug on the dark wooden floor.

'Do you think everything was Dad's fault?' said Tori.

'It was circumstances,' I said wisely, which was

something I'd heard said on (the new) telly the night before.

'I suppose,' Tori said.

We padded down the sunlight-striped stairs to look in on Mum and say Happy Christmas. She was sitting up in bed and staring out of the window, over the top of the little cot where Grandpa was sleeping. When she saw us peeping round the door, she quickly swiped away the tears on her cheeks and tried to smile.

'Happy Christmas, *queridas*.'

'We miss him too, Mum,' said Tori as I rushed in and wrapped Mum in a big hug.

'He'll come back,' I said, feeling a bit tearful myself.

'No,' Mum gulped. 'I don't think that he will.'

'Well, that's cheerful for Christmas Day,' I said, letting go a bit indignantly. 'Think positive, Mum! This time last week we never thought we'd be waking up in a house in the middle of Wild World, with you having a proper zoo job and Grandpa snoozing in a wicked little cot all of his own, did we?'

'And we didn't think we'd have new furniture or a TV with a special sci-fi channel we could pick up either, did we?' Tori added.

Mum gave a watery smile. 'You are right of course, darlings. I must be positive, mustn't I?'

'I'll go downstairs and make some toast,' I said.

'With the new toaster,' added Tori.

'And a cup of coffee . . .'

'With the new kettle and new mugs . . .'

'And some orange juice . . .'

'From the new fridge . . .'

'And find that nice new tray we bought to put it on and bring it back up here, shall I?' I finished. 'We can all have breakfast in your bed.'

Grandpa yawned and sat up, rubbing his eyes just like a baby does. I left Tori and Mum cuddling him and padded downstairs, pushing open the kitchen door and stroking Rabbit as she frantically looked around for something to bring me. I fed her, then switched the kettle on and pushed open the kitchen window. Faint sounds of yelping wild animals drifted in on the cold Christmas air while the kettle boiled. I made the coffee, poured three glasses of juice and put down the toast. Then, mainly because I could, I went into the sitting room and switched on the new flat-screen telly that sat on the new telly cabinet in the corner. Well, Christmas isn't Christmas without a bit of Christmas telly, is it?

I yelped with shock as the macaques swam across the screen, their tails held up out of the water and mist drifting behind them. *Already?* Boy, those telly guys had been quick.

'TORI!' I screamed. 'MUM! The macaques are on TV!'

The camera panned over Fatso, water trembling on the whiskery bits on the side of his chubby face just as Tori and Mum came thundering down the stairs. Tiny's tail disappeared off the screen and the link morphed into the opening credits for *Mary Poppins* as they skidded into the sitting room. Slung over Mum's shoulder, Grandpa *whoomph*ed in a puzzled sort of way.

'Where?' demanded Tori breathlessly.

I waved at the TV. 'Missed it,' I explained, still reeling from the wonderful shock. It had all been over in ten seconds flat. All that effort, I thought in amazement, for just ten seconds. TV was a strange, strange world. 'It'll be on again after the film, I expect.'

Tori stared in horror at *Mary Poppins*. 'Do we have to watch this soppy film all the way through till they show it again?'

'They might not show it straight after,' I said. 'We might have to watch TV *all day long* just to be sure to see it again.' I glanced hopefully at Mum. We'd never been allowed to watch TV all day long, but for the macaques maybe Mum would make an exception.

'You can watch until they repeat the link,' Mum said, smiling as I fell on the sofa with a squeal of bliss. 'Now I'm taking my coffee and Grandpa back to bed.'

The doorbell went. Mum stopped halfway up the stairs as Tori opened the door.

Dad was standing on the porch. He held two plastic bags, shiny wrapping paper and ribbons peeping out.

'Happy Christmas, everyone,' he said with a nervous smile. 'Can I come in?'